"I *am not* hyst[...]
Phyllida. "I'm [...]

"I know, and your feet hurt," Jake interrupted her unsympathetically. "If you stopped thinking about them, they wouldn't hurt nearly so much."

"And if you knew how much they hurt, you wouldn't even suggest thinking about anything else," she retorted.

"You must be able to think of something that'll stop you feeling so sorry for yourself," he said, reluctant amusement creeping back into his voice.

"You suggest something, if you're so clever," snapped Phyllida.

"All right," said Jake equably, and calmly took her in his arms. "How about this?"

Phyllida was taken completely unawares and toppled against him, clutching automatically at his chest as he bent his head and kissed her.

Dear Reader,

Help us celebrate life, love and happy-ever-afters with our great new series.

Everybody loves a party and birthday parties best of all, so join some of your favorite authors and celebrate in style with seven fantastic new romances. One for every day of the week, in fact, and each featuring a truly wonderful woman whose story fits the lines of the old rhyme "Monday's child is..."

> Monday's child is fair of face,
> Tuesday's child is full of grace,
> Wednesday's child is full of woe,
> Thursday's child has far to go,
> Friday's child is loving and giving,
> Saturday's child works hard for its living,
> And a child that's born on a Sunday,
> Is bonny and blithe and good and gay.

(Anon.)

Does the day on which you're born affect your character? Some people think so—if you want to find out more, read our exciting new series. Available wherever Harlequin books are sold:

May	#3407	The Marriage Business	Jessica Steele
June	#3412	Private Dancer	Eva Rutland
July	#3417	Coming Home	Patricia Wilson
August	#3422	Desperately Seeking Annie	Patricia Knoll
September	#3424	A Simple Texas Wedding	Ruth Jean Dale
October	#3429	Working Girl	Jessica Hart
November	#3434	Dream Wedding	Helen Brooks

Happy reading,

The Editors, Harlequin Romance

Working Girl
Jessica Hart

Harlequin Books

TORONTO • NEW YORK • LONDON
AMSTERDAM • PARIS • SYDNEY • HAMBURG
STOCKHOLM • ATHENS • TOKYO • MILAN
MADRID • WARSAW • BUDAPEST • AUCKLAND

For Ali and Fully

ISBN 0-373-03429-6

WORKING GIRL

First North American Publication 1996.

Printed in U.S.A.

CHAPTER ONE

IT WAS like running into a rock.

'Ouf!' Head down, struggling with her heavy suitcase, Phyllida didn't notice the man heading for the same terminal door until she cannoned into him. She hadn't known that a man's body could feel so solid.

The force of the impact drove the breath from her lungs, and she staggered back and would have tripped over her suitcase if a hand hadn't shot out to catch her and set her back on her feet.

'Careful!' The iron grip on her arm relaxed as Phyllida recovered her balance and looked up to find a man regarding her frowningly.

He was deeply tanned, with brown hair and a cool, watchful face, and her first thought was that he was not as big as he had seemed when she had run into the powerful body. Its strength was unmistakable, but kept compact and very controlled. Her second was that he looked distinctly unfriendly.

'Don't you think it would be an idea to look where you're going with that thing?' he said, nodding down at the huge suitcase, which had toppled over onto its side. His voice managed to be deep and cool at the same time.

Phyllida, who had opened her mouth to apologise, felt unaccountably ruffled. She was still jarred and breathless from the collision, and she rubbed her arm where he had gripped her.

'I'm in a hurry,' she said, rather more sharply than she had intended. But, after all, *he* hadn't apologised for running into *her* had he? 'I didn't see you.'

'Obviously not.'

The sardonic note in his voice made her glance up from her arm, and her heart jerked strangely as she found herself looking into his eyes. They were a dark, guarded green, almost grey, and disconcertingly observant.

Phyllida was suddenly conscious of how she must look. She had been travelling for over thirty-seven hours, and was sure that she looked as tired and crumpled as she felt. Her cream and white suit, which had looked so smart in London, was irretrievably creased, and the gold shoes which matched her belt were pinching painfully at her swollen feet.

Phyllida wasn't a tall girl, but usually there was a dynamism about her that more than made up for her lack of inches. Unfortunately, this man with his faintly contemptuous gaze would be hard put to it to spot any dynamism at the moment. All he would see was that she was short and flustered, and that her face was bright red after the race between the terminals.

He could probably see that the backs of her tights were badly laddered, too. He had that sort of look about him.

'My plane from London only landed a few minutes ago,' she found herself explaining. 'We were hours late, but someone said I might be just in time to catch the last flight to Port Lincoln if I hurried. I've just run all the way from the international terminal...' She tailed off. Why was she telling him all this? He wasn't interested in her nightmare journey.

She glanced distractedly at her watch. Eight-forty. The flight was due to leave in five minutes.

'In that case, how inconsiderate of me to get in your way,' said the man.

There was something in his voice, an undercurrent of derision, that made Phyllida's hackles rise. Typical man—superior, patronising, determined to make a woman feel unreasonable, whatever she did! She had had enough of men like that recently. It was just her luck that the first man she came across in Australia had to conform to type!

Lips tightening, she bent to set her case back on its wheels. She was supposed to be able to pull it along behind her, but it kept slewing sideways, scraping itself down the back of her legs as it did so. Her tights were ruined and her ankles would be black and blue tomorrow.

Phyllida had learned to hate the wheels with a deep and passionate loathing since she had left her flat. Unfortunately, the case was too heavy for her to carry any other way.

The man was watching her struggle to right it. Leaning down with a muttered exclamation, he made to lift the case, but Phyllida had heard the irritable click of the tongue, and it only seemed to confirm her opinion of him. He was just like all the rest—convinced that a woman couldn't do anything for herself.

'I can manage!' she snapped, glaring at him.

'You don't look as if you're managing very well,' he pointed out, with that same hatefully sardonic edge. 'Wouldn't it make life easier if you travelled with a case that wasn't almost as big as you are?'

Phyllida's chin came up at his sarcasm. 'I may be small, but it doesn't mean my brain is!' she said defiantly. 'Why do men always think women are incapable of looking after themselves? I've managed to get myself to the other side of the world without some patronising man telling me how I ought to travel or how much I need to pack.'

As if to prove her point, she managed to haul the case up with a grunt of effort. She shot him a look of triumph. 'See? I can cope quite well by myself!'

The man was unimpressed. 'It looks more like struggling than coping to me,' he said. 'Personally, I'd have preferred to have had a chance of catching my plane than to try and prove a point. But if you think you can get that case to the check-in desk just as quickly by yourself, you'd better carry on—and if you want to catch the Port Lincoln flight, I should forget about your principles and hurry!'

'That's precisely what I was doing,' said Phyllida frostily. Still breathing hard, she took hold of the lead. In theory, the case was supposed to glide along behind you, like a particularly well-behaved dog, but it never seemed to work like that in practice.

'Now, if you'll excuse me?' she added, with awful politeness. But her grand manner didn't really fit the small, slight figure in the crumpled suit, and a disturbing gleam of amusement sprang into the grey-green eyes.

'Of course,' he said, with equally insincere politeness.

Humiliatingly certain that he found her ridiculous, Phyllida stuck her chin in the air and tried to stalk off towards the row of check-in desks, but her dignified departure was ruined by the fact that she had only taken two steps before the case promptly toppled over again.

Betrayed into an extremely unladylike word, Phyllida wrestled it upright again, very conscious of the man's cool, amused eyes on her back. Her cheeks burned with mortification, and an obscure conviction that it was somehow all his fault.

The case fell over twice before she reached the check-in desks, and by then, of course, it was too late anyway. The young official behind the counter was sympathetic, but positive. The flight had gone, and there wouldn't be another to Port Lincoln until the following day.

Phyllida had known she was too late, but she had been hoping against hope that this flight would be delayed—like every other one on her marathon journey from London—and the knowledge that she had missed it by minutes only made things worse.

She slumped against the check-in desk in despair. She was beginning to wish that she'd never decided to come to Australia. Her rushed departure, the long delays and missed connections, the cramped conditions and ghastly food, the two-year-old across the aisle who had screamed for hours on end... She had gritted her teeth and endured them all, promising herself that it would all be worth it when she got to Port Lincoln.

Chris and Mike would be there, and they would welcome her in, and she could throw her hateful suitcase to the back of a wardrobe and forget about it for three months. Phyllida had set her heart on being there that night, and the news that her arrival would have to be delayed yet again brought her close to tears of exhaustion and sheer frustration.

Out of the corner of her eye, she could see the man she had bumped into at the terminal door. She wouldn't have been able to catch the flight anyway, so it was quite illogical to blame him for the fact that she had missed it, but Phyllida still eyed him with resentment.

He was chatting to an airline official a few yards away, looking infuriatingly cool and assured. Phyllida wished she felt like that. She wondered where he was going. He was wearing beautifully cut trousers and a short-sleeved shirt and tie, so understated they had to be expensive. His only luggage was an equally discreet leather briefcase, so he couldn't be going far.

Was he going back to a home, a family? There was something self-contained about him that made it hard to imagine him surrounded by wife and children, she decided, then abruptly changed her mind as he smiled at something his companion had said.

The effect was totally unexpected, dissolving the guarded expression into warmth and humour and softening the rather hard lines of his face. Even from some distance away Phyllida could see how white his teeth were against his tan, and she felt as if she had run into him all over again. Why hadn't she seen what an attractive man he was before?

Stunned by the transformation, Phyllida had momentarily forgotten her own situation, but as she stared he looked over unexpectedly, and across the empty terminal their eyes met with a jolting sensation. His expression was unnervingly keen, and Phyllida stiffened, only too aware of how she must appear, slumped wearily against the counter. She was sure she could read mockery in those grey-green eyes. He was probably remembering her proud boast that she could manage perfectly well by herself.

And so she could. Phyllida straightened. She had decided to arrive in Port Lincoln tonight, and she would get there if it killed her—if only to prove that she could to the stranger with the unsettling eyes and the unexpected smile. The fact that he would never know if she succeeded was forgotten. All that mattered was showing him that she wouldn't let herself be beaten by anything!

She smiled appealingly at the young man behind the desk. In spite of her tiredness, there was still some bounce in the glossy nut-brown hair that was cut in a short bob to frame a gamine face with a pert nose and a pair of wide, expressive brown eyes.

'Isn't there *any* way I can get to Port Lincoln tonight?' she pleaded, and let him see the shimmer of tears in her eyes.

Few men were proof against Phyllida's wide brown gaze. 'I really am sorry,' he said regretfully. 'But unless—' He broke off as he caught sight of someone over her shoulder.

'You might be in luck after all!' He grinned. 'That's Jake Tregowan. He flies his own plane, and it looks as if he's heading back to Port Lincoln now. If you asked him, I'm sure he'd give you a lift.' He waved an arm. 'Jake! Have you got a moment?'

Even before she turned, something told Phyllida who Jake Tregowan would be.

It was him. Of course it was him. He was walking towards them with a deliberate, unhurried tread, the disconcerting eyes alight with mockery as they rested on her face.

Phyllida's heart sank. Why did it have to be him? The one person who could help her; the one person she couldn't ask. She winced as she remembered how she had scorned his help with her case, had boasted about the fact that she didn't need a man to get from A to B.

Jake was exchanging greetings with the young man behind the desk. He seemed to be on first-name terms with everyone here, she thought sourly. He must spend his whole time at the airport. He was standing a couple of feet away, but she could sense the coiled power of his body as if it were pressed against her.

The thought made her shiver. Jake glanced towards her, one brow raised enquiringly.

'This lady's plane from England was delayed, and she's missed her connection,' her champion explained. 'She's very anxious to get to Port Lincoln tonight. Are you on your way back there now?'

'Yes,' said Jake, deliberately ignoring his cue to offer her a lift.

Phyllida bit her lip. She couldn't really blame him, not after all she had had to say before. Tiredness washed over her. She didn't want to swallow her pride and beg him for a lift; she didn't want to go anywhere with him. What she really wanted to do was sit down and cry, but she couldn't do that—not with him watching her with that sardonic expression of his.

And she *did* want to get to Port Lincoln. If she could just get to Chris and Mike, everything would be all right. She had reached the point where that was all that mattered.

Clenching her jaw, Phyllida pressed the betraying waver of her lips fiercely together and looked Jake straight in the eye. 'My name's Phyllida Grant,' she said with some difficulty. 'If you're flying to Port Lincoln, I'd be very grateful if you'd take me with you.'

'Surely you don't mean you want some help after all?' he mocked. 'I thought you were quite capable of getting yourself to Port Lincoln without any patronising male assistance?'

Phyllida gritted her teeth. 'I would have been if I hadn't missed the last flight,' she said.

'And that was presumably my fault, for letting myself be run into?'

'No,' she admitted honestly. 'I was too late anyway.' She pushed her fringe off her forehead, leaving the shiny brown hair sticking out at different angles like a small child's.

She was wondering if she should try to explain that the collision in the doors had just been the culmination of a series of small disasters that had begun six weeks ago, when she had lost her job and thrown Rupert's ring back in his face. Nothing had gone right since then, but Phyllida had carried on doggedly, refusing to let herself be beaten by circumstance.

Looking at Jake Tregowan's cool, guarded features, she didn't think he would understand. Things would never dare go wrong for him. In the end, she simply passed her hand over her face in an age-old gesture of weariness. 'It's been a long trip,' was all she said.

Jake looked at her, a small, tense figure standing by her huge suitcase. She wasn't a beautiful girl, but the wide brown eyes, tilted nose and curving mouth had a charm and piquancy of their own, and there was something gallant in the stubborn way she was keeping the tears at bay. She looked defiant, determined . . . and very tired.

He sighed. 'You'd better come with me,' he said resignedly.

'Thank you,' said Phyllida, a little wary of his sudden change in attitude, but too relieved at the prospect of getting to Port Lincoln to ask why.

'I'm leaving right now,' he warned, as if regretting his decision already.

'That's all right.' She reached down for her suitcase. 'I'm ready.'

'Let's go, then.' Jake strode off without another word, leaving Phyllida to thank the young official behind the counter for his help and hurry after him.

She was hampered as usual by her wretched case, which lurched from side to side no matter how carefully she pulled it. She was very aware of Jake, who had halted impatiently and was watching her awkward progress with an expression of barely disguised exasperation. He hadn't offered to carry her case, and there was no way she was going to ask him, Phyllida told herself. Swallowing her pride over the lift had been bad enough.

'Ouch!' She hadn't been concentrating, and the case had keeled over, raking one corner down the back of her legs before falling with a heavy thud that echoed down the empty corridor.

'You appear to be having some difficulty,' said Jake. 'Or is this another example of you coping by yourself?'

Phyllida had been rubbing her calf, but now she aimed a childish kick at the case. 'It's supposed to run along on wheels,' she complained, with a venomous look at it. 'But they keep swivelling round so that it can savage the back of my legs.' She twisted her leg round so that he could see the full extent of the damage. 'Look, my tights are ruined!'

Jake wasn't interested in her laddered tights. 'There's no point in blaming the case,' he said astringently. 'It's not designed to take that kind of weight. If you'd packed less, it might work better.'

'I had to leave half my clothes behind as it was,' Phyllida grumbled. 'What's the point in having a case if you can't fill it?'

'What's the point in having a case you can't carry?' he retorted as she struggled to lift it up from the floor.

'I *can*—' Phyllida began to protest, jaw clenched with effort as she heaved at the case. But she was interrupted by Jake's exclamation of impatience.

Putting her aside with hard hands, he took the case from her. 'You can't carry it, can you?'

Phyllida looked at the floor. 'No,' she muttered.

'Pardon?'

'No, I can't carry it!' she shouted, provoked just as he had intended. 'It's too heavy and I wish I had brought a smaller one.' She glared at him. 'There! Satisfied now, or would you like me to write it out fifty times and sign every page in triplicate?'

Jake looked down at her. He wasn't exactly smiling, but the cool eyes were gleaming with humour, and the crease at the corner of his mouth had deepened almost imperceptibly. 'Haven't you ever heard of giving in graciously?'

'I don't like giving in.' Phyllida's chin was set at a stubborn angle, and Jake eyed her with amusement as he bent to pick up the case.

'You might have to learn to get used to it,' he said.

Phyllida watched resentfully as he carried her case with perfect ease. It might as well have been empty for all the strain it showed in the muscles of his arms, and she found herself remembering again how strong and solid his body had been when she had bumped against him. The memory was uncomfortably vivid.

Jake kicked open a swing-door and held it open for her with his foot. Outside, a row of small planes was parked on the tarmac, and Phyllida trailed past after him to where a tiny plane with a propeller on its nose stood at the end of the line. Jake pulled open the door in its side, threw in her case, and then swung himself easily up after it.

Phyllida stopped dead, appalled at the sight of the flimsy little plane. 'We're not going in *that*?'

'What were you expecting? Concorde?'

'I thought you'd have your own jet,' she said, confused. It was the only kind of private plane she had ever come across before.

'A private jet would be very nice, but a touch ostentatious for flying between Port Lincoln and Adelaide,' said Jake drily. 'This is more than adequate.'

She looked doubtfully at the propeller. 'It's not very... *big*, is it?'

'It can take four people if necessary, so it should be quite big enough for you, me and even your suitcase. Of course,' he added, 'you can stay behind and catch a flight tomorrow morning if you prefer. It won't make any difference to me.'

'No,' said Phyllida quickly. She wasn't going to turn back when she was this close to Port Lincoln. 'I mean, I'd like to come, thank you.'

Jake reached a hand down from the doorway. 'Well, if you're going to come, come on!'

Phyllida looked up at him. The doorway was about level with her shoulder. 'Haven't you got any steps?'

'No,' he said bluntly. 'There are some steps back in the terminal, but if you think I'm going to go back and get them for you, you've got another think coming!'

'How am I supposed to get in, then?'

'You've got arms and legs, haven't you? Just take my hand and climb up!'

'Climb? I'd need a pole vault to get up there!'

'Don't be ridiculous,' said Jake, his patience rapidly running out. 'It's perfectly easy. Here, take my hand.'

He reached down, and Phyllida took his hand reluctantly, conscious of a strange jolt of reaction all the way down her spine as his fingers closed firmly around hers. They were warm and strong and infinitely reassuring, and she looked at their linked hands in surprise that she could feel so much from a simple clasp.

Jake sighed. 'I don't know about you, Phyllida, but I've got better things to do than stand here all night holding hands. Now, if you want to stay here in Adelaide, that's fine by me. But if you want to come to Port Lincoln, then hurry up and get on with it!'

Phyllida did try. She managed to get one arm and a shoulder onto the floor of the plane, while Jake hauled on the other one, but her legs flailed around hopelessly, hampered by her short skirt, and in the end she fell back, panting with humiliation.

'I told you I couldn't get up there,' she gasped. 'I'm not Superwoman!'

'That's not the impression you were giving earlier on,' Jake pointed out with some acidity. 'Although if you were as capable as you claimed, you wouldn't even have considered travelling in a skirt like that.'

'Had I known that I was going to be taking part in an obstacle course, I would have worn my tracksuit!' snapped Phyllida, forgetting for a moment that she was quite dependent on Jake Tregowan's good nature if she wanted to get to Port Lincoln tonight. She brushed at the sleeve of her jacket, where she had clung to the floor of the plane. 'As it is, this suit will never be the same again!'

Muttering under his breath, Jake jumped out of the plane and landed lightly beside her. 'Frankly, your suit is the least of my worries at the moment,' he said. He glanced from Phyllida to the plane, as if judging the distance, then put his hands to her waist and hoisted her bodily up towards the door.

Phyllida squeaked in surprise at finding herself suddenly grabbed, but managed to clutch at the opening. She was very aware of the hard hands at her waist, hands that slid impersonally down her legs as he pushed her up until she could collapse in an inelegant heap inside the plane.

For a long moment she just lay there, gasping like a landed fish and wondering what on earth she was doing sprawled on the floor of some tinpot aeroplane with a disagreeable stranger stepping over her as if she was of no more importance than a sack of potatoes—which was exactly what she felt like.

'Welcome aboard,' said Jake, with an unmistakable edge of dry amusement.

Phyllida struggled wearily into a sitting position and looked down at her filthy hands. 'British Airways was never like this,' she sighed, and Jake's mouth twitched into a smile—the same devastating smile that she had noticed across the terminal. His teeth gleamed in the dim light as he reached down and helped her to her feet with what she was sure was mock gallantry.

'Service is everything,' he said.

Phyllida took her hand from his rather quickly, alarmed by the way all the nerves down her spine seemed to shiver whenever he touched her. His smile made her edgy. It wasn't at all the sort of smile she would have expected him to have. He should have a cool, contained smile to go with his cool, contained image. Not a smile with this warmth that tugged at her own mouth in response even as it dried the breath in her throat.

She dragged her eyes away from it with an effort. Desperate for a distraction, she looked around her with spurious interest, but his smile still danced tantalisingly in front of her eyes. She had to shake her head to banish it. 'Where's the pilot?' she asked, once she could see properly again.

'You seem to have very strange ideas of my grandeur, Phyllida,' said Jake drily, pointing her towards the co-pilot's seat. 'I hate to disappoint you, but not only do I not have a private jet, I don't have a pilot waiting on my convenience either.'

'You mean, you fly yourself?'

'Why not?'

'I just assumed...' She trailed off, feeling foolish.

'Assumed what? That I was incapable of flying a plane?'

'No!' Jake Tregowan didn't look incapable of *any-thing*. 'I suppose I thought you looked successful enough to have someone to fly it for you.'

He watched critically as she strapped herself in, then settled into the pilot's seat beside her. 'What made you think that?'

It was the way he walked, the way he turned his head—even the way he stood, looking cool and decisive. Phyllida didn't think she could tell Jake any of that. 'Just the clothes you were wearing,' she said lamely.

'That's a big assumption to base on a pair of trousers and a shirt,' he commented, with one of his sardonic looks. 'Do you always leap to conclusions like that?'

'I wasn't that far wrong, was I?' she challenged him. 'You're obviously successful enough to have your own plane, anyway.'

'Australia's a big country.' He shrugged as the propeller coughed and started to turn, slowly at first and then with increasing speed, but she noticed that he didn't deny it. 'Flying is often the best way to get around.'

He began checking his instrument panel while Phyllida watched the propeller rather nervously. She had never been in anything smaller than a jumbo before, and she was beginning to regret asking Jake for a lift. Really, she would have done much better to have stayed in Adelaide, where she would have been able to have a good night's sleep. She could have showered and changed into clean clothes, and arrived in Port Lincoln refreshed.

As it was, she was going to turn up on Chris's doorstep looking a total wreck. Why hadn't she thought of that before?

Phyllida looked down at her smudged and rumpled suit, and repressed a sigh as she remembered what Jake had said about leaping to conclusions. She liked to think of herself as businesslike and professional, but the truth was that she had always been too impetuous, with a tendency towards snap decisions and making a bee-line for what she wanted without stopping to think about what was involved.

She glanced across at Jake, absorbed in his instruments. She couldn't imagine *him* ever acting without thinking. He was too deliberate, too controlled. Her eyes fell on his hands, reaching up to the panel above his head, moving competently over the switches with the minimum of fuss, and an unidentifiable feeling gripped the base of her spine.

Rupert would have flourished his arms about, impressing her with his knowledge, Phyllida thought wryly. He wouldn't have just sat there ignoring her, as Jake was doing, working steadily through his routine.

She frowned slightly as she realised that she couldn't quite visualise Rupert's face. She had been engaged to him until that disastrous afternoon six weeks ago. Surely she couldn't have forgotten him in that time? Closing her eyes, she made an effort to conjure up his image. But all she could see was Jake's watchful eyes and Jake's cool mouth and Jake's disturbing smile.

'Right.' His voice broke into her thoughts. 'Ready?'

Phyllida looked at the propeller again and swallowed. 'I suppose so.' It was too late to change her mind now, but next time she really *would* think before she rushed into a decision.

They waited while a jet landed with a roar at the international terminal, and then they were speeding down the runway. Phyllida kept her eyes squeezed shut and clutched her hands together as the pressure forced her back into her seat.

The lurch of her stomach told her that the plane had left the ground, but she kept her eyes firmly closed until the plane's steep climb into the air had levelled off. When she opened them, Jake was watching her with a mixture of amusement and exasperation.

'Wishing you'd waited for tomorrow morning's flight after all?'

Phyllida's chin went up at the mockery in his voice. 'No,' she lied, and a smile touched the corners of his mouth.

'Stubborn little thing, aren't you?'

She thought of the determination she had needed to succeed in her advertising career, and how little it had counted when set against the fact that she was female. She would show them, though! 'Sometimes you have to be,' she said.

'What's made you so stubborn about getting to Port Lincoln?' Jake asked, guiding the plane round in a wide arc.

Phyllida looked down at the lights of Adelaide spread out below her and swallowed. 'I just wanted to get there tonight.'

'And what you want, you get—regardless of inconvenience to other people?'

She glanced at him curiously, wondering what had provoked the bitterness in his voice. 'No,' she said slowly, thinking of the day her world had fallen apart and she had lost her job and her fiancé in the course of a single afternoon. 'Not always.'

'Oh?' Jake's eyes flicked towards her in disbelief. 'I had you down as a real career girl in your smart suit.'

His voice was edged with sudden contempt, and Phyllida stiffened. 'I thought it was dangerous to base assumptions on what people were wearing?' she reminded him.

'I was going by the way you behaved, not by what you were wearing—typically unsuitable though it is,' he retorted. 'All fragile and feminine when it suits you, but hard as nails underneath.'

'What do you mean?' said Phyllida, offended.

'Oh, come on, I saw the way you were making up to that poor unsuspecting boy at the check-in desk! Opening those big brown eyes of yours at him, bravely choking back a few tears... it was quite a performance! Unfortunately, I've seen it all before, and I know that the performance only ever lasts as long as it takes to get your own way. You're full of fine words about not needing men, but you don't mind using them when it suits you, do you?'

Phyllida's face was white with anger. 'And what about the men who use women?' she demanded. 'It's all right for them to make the most of our talents and abilities, but as soon as we start asking for some acknowledgement, that's another matter!

'We're only supposed to be there to support men, to fill in time before we run back to our proper place as housekeepers and mothers. Do you have any idea how hard it is for a woman to get to the top of her career?' she asked him furiously.

'You have to work twice as hard as any man to get taken seriously. Instead of getting on with the job, you have to prove that you can be just as ruthless as your male colleagues, and when you are, they turn round and accuse you of being hard and unfeminine! But of course we're not allowed to be feminine either, because that's unfair to men!' Phyllida paused for breath, brown eyes bright with indignation.

'The only way you can succeed is by being utterly determined to beat all the odds, but it shouldn't be that hard. Women are just as capable as men. Why shouldn't we have the same opportunities to be successful and show what we can do?'

'Very vehement,' said Jake, with an ironic sidelong glance. 'I was obviously right about you being a career girl, anyway.'

'Yes, I am,' she said defiantly. 'And proud of it!'

'What do you do?'

'I'm in advertising.'

'How can you be proud of being in advertising?' he asked nastily.

'Easily,' said Phyllida, determinedly dignified. 'Our advertising affects the way people think about almost everything, and we take our responsibility very seriously. It's a very professional business.'

She would have gone on, but at that moment Jake took his hands off the joystick and settled himself back in his seat. To her horror, he proceeded to shift himself into a more comfortable position and calmly propped his legs up against the instrument panel.

'What are you doing?' she asked, her voice rising to an extremely unprofessional squeak.

Jake gave an irritable sigh. 'We're on autopilot. There's no need to panic.'

'I wasn't panicking,' said Phyllida coldly. She hated the way Jake Tregowan made her feel stupid. 'I was just...concerned.'

'I should keep your concern for a society subjected to a barrage of pointless advertising, if I were you,' said Jake, and forestalled her protest by reaching behind his seat to pull out a Thermos flask.

As he unscrewed the top a tantalising aroma of fresh coffee drifted out into the cockpit, distracting Phyllida from her dignified and well-reasoned arguments in favour of advertising. Her nose twitched. She had last eaten at thirty thousand feet, somewhere between Singapore and Adelaide, and it seemed a very long time ago.

'Want some?' he asked, filling the top which doubled as a mug.

The smell was irresistible. 'I'd love some,' she admitted, abandoning her dignity along with her arguments. Her swollen feet were killing her, and she grimaced with relief as she eased off her shoes.

Jake handed her the mug. Her fingers brushed against his as she took it from him, and her grateful smile faltered slightly at the electric effect of his touch.

Clasping her hands around the mug, she tried to concentrate fiercely on the coffee, but her eyes kept sliding sideways to study him from under her lashes. They rested on his profile, on the strong features lit from below by the dim lights of the instruments, caught on the set of his jaw and the peculiarly exciting line of his mouth, and something stirred strangely inside her.

She must be even more tired than she'd thought, Phyllida decided. There was something vaguely surreal about sitting here in the darkness, high above the ground, drinking coffee with a perfect stranger while the propeller droned mesmerisingly in the background. Only Jake seemed real. Real and solid and somehow *immediate*.

Even in the dim light, everything about him was distinct. She could sense the muscles in the legs bent so casually against the instrument panel, the strength in the lean, compact body, could almost feel the texture of his skin. So vivid was the sensation that Phyllida had to look down at her fingers, to make sure that they weren't in fact exploring the angle of his cheek and jaw.

She wished she couldn't remember every time he had touched her. The steely grip on her arm, setting her back on her feet, his hand clasping hers to haul her into the plane, the hard hold at her waist... Her body throbbed as if every touch had seared into her skin. If a brief, impersonal contact could feel like this, what would it be like if he touched her lovingly, running his hands over her skin, exploring her softness...?

Phyllida's throat dried at the thought, and she gulped at the last of the coffee. What on earth was the matter with her? She hardly knew Jake Tregowan, and what she did know she didn't like. Why could she picture him making love to her with such alarming clarity?

Jet lag, she told herself firmly. Her mind was confused and disorientated by the long flight, just as her body was. Phyllida grasped at the explanation with something akin to desperation. It meant that there was a perfectly logical reason for the sudden, heart-stopping rush of desire, and that it had nothing—absolutely nothing!—to do with Jake Tregowan.

CHAPTER TWO

SHE handed him back the mug, careful not to touch him this time. 'Thank you.'

Jake raised his brows at the strained formality of her tone, but to Phyllida's relief he didn't comment. Instead he poured himself some coffee from the Thermos. 'What are you doing in Port Lincoln?' he asked, with that undercurrent of mockery that so riled her. 'I wouldn't have thought it was exactly the mecca of the advertising world. Or have you got some brief to jazz up our international image?'

'I'm on a three-month sabbatical,' said Phyllida. She had no intention of telling Jake Tregowan that the job she had loved so much was no longer hers.

'Sabbatical? Isn't that what the rest of us would call a holiday?'

'I'm taking a long break from work to give me a chance to reassess my career,' she said grandly. It was almost the truth, anyway.

'Port Lincoln seems a funny place to choose to do that,' Jake commented, watching her over the rim of the mug. 'I thought you career girls only ever did things that looked good on your CVs?'

Phyllida eyed him with some hostility. 'You seem to know a lot about career girls.'

'I've learnt from bitter experience,' he said flatly.

'Your experience can't be that wide if it hasn't taught you that we're not all the same,' she pointed out in a tart voice. 'For your information, I'm going to visit my cousin, not add to my CV.'

'Aha! So you *are* on holiday!'

'Partly,' she admitted through clenched teeth. 'Of course I want to see Chris again, but I wouldn't be here now unless it was a good time as far as my firm was concerned.'

'If they can spare you for three months, they probably don't need you at all,' said Jake with disagreeable logic. 'Are you sure you're going to have a job when you get back?'

She lifted her chin. 'Not only will I have a job, I'm going to be promoted,' she said proudly.

And she would. Liedermann, Marshall & Jones would regret giving her job to someone who was less experienced and less qualified, but who operated under the enormous advantage of being male. Phyllida had vowed that day to make them come crawling back on their knees and beg her to accept promotion, and she had dreamt of it so often that it had come to seem almost an established fact.

'And in the meantime you're going to spend three months in Port Lincoln thinking about things?' Jake's voice was edged with disbelief.

'Yes,' said Phyllida firmly. She had a nasty suspicion that Jake was less than convinced about her impressive career. 'I'll go and see other parts of Australia, but I'll be quite happy to spend most of my time with Chris,' she went on, anxious to prevent him asking any more awkward questions about her career and just why it was that she could take three months off right now.

To her relief, Jake allowed himself to be diverted. 'That's your cousin?'

She nodded. 'Her father—my mother's brother—emigrated to Australia years ago and married an Australian. I'd only ever heard about Chris through letters until she and her husband came to England on a working holiday. They stayed with me in London and we hit it off immediately.' She smiled reminiscently.

'It was wonderful to discover a friend instead of just a relative. We've kept in touch ever since, although I haven't seen them for five years now. It's such a long way that I've never thought about coming out before.'

'What made you change your mind?'

'Chris sent me a photograph.' Phyllida dug in her bag for it. She had carried it around like a talisman ever since Chris's letter had dropped through the door along with a pile of Christmas cards.

Her fingers found the picture tucked into the back of her passport, and she pulled it out to look down at it again in the dim light. It showed Chris and Mike on a boat, sharply outlined in the bright Australia light. They both looked relaxed and happy, with the wind lifting their hair and the sun making them screw up their eyes. It was hard to tell now, but behind them the sea was an unreal shade of turquoise, the sky a deep, bright blue.

She passed the photograph across to Jake, who glanced at it and stiffened suddenly. Phyllida didn't notice. She was remembering how miserable she had been feeling when she had first seen it. 'I know it's just an ordinary snapshot, but it arrived on a horrible December day. It was drizzling, and everything looked wet and grey and...I don't know...*dreary*.'

'I can see that this would have looked more appealing,' said Jake. There was an odd note in his voice as he handed her back the photograph.

'Maybe if it had arrived on a bright, frosty day, it wouldn't have meant so much,' Phyllida said reflectively. The snapshot had seemed so vivid. She had practically been able to feel the sunshine on her back, and smell the fresh, sharp tang of the sea.

'I've always been a real city girl, but when I looked at it, I suddenly wanted to be there with them.' She had wanted to leave the greyness behind and forget about her job, forget about Rupert, forget about everything but the bright light and the sea spray on her face.

'And you just happened to have a three-month sabbatical coming up, is that it?' Jake didn't even bother to hide his sarcasm, and Phyllida flushed, glad that the light wasn't good enough for him to tell.

'More or less,' she said stiffly. 'I hadn't really decided what I was going to do.' Until then, she hadn't thought beyond a single-minded determination to prove both LMJ and Rupert wrong, but Chris's letter with its usual warm invitation to visit had changed that.

There was no reason why she shouldn't go to Australia, she had realised. She had been earning a good salary, and had worked so hard that she had never had the time to spend much of it. She had no commitments—no ties since she had stormed out of Rupert's flat. Instead of plodding through a grim, grey January, she could lie in the sun and come home tanned and refreshed and ready to prove herself again.

'I could have gone anywhere, but the photograph made me realise what a perfect opportunity it was to see Chris and Mike again.'

'They look fairly cheerful types,' he commented lightly.

Phyllida's face changed. 'They were *then*. Whether they will be now is another matter.'

'Oh?' He shot her a swift glance. 'Why's that?'

'Mike's always been a restless type, but he and Chris had finally settled down to what they really wanted to do, which was run a marine charter company, hiring out their two yachts. It was only a small business, but at least it was theirs—until some rival company comes along and decides it can't tolerate a little fair competition!'

Phyllida sat straighter, remembering her indignation as she had read Chris's letter telling her about the takeover.

'Chris and Mike wouldn't have been a threat to anybody, but that didn't make any difference to the man who took them over. All *he* cares about is profit. He doesn't care that they've put all their effort, not to mention all their savings into making their business a success. People don't matter to men like that,' she said bitterly. 'They just brush aside anyone who stands in their way!'

'I had no idea there was such a ruthless operator in Port Lincoln,' said Jake. 'Did your cousin tell you his name, so I can take care to avoid him in future?' His face was quite grave, but Phyllida had the distinct impression that he was amused by something.

She glared at him. It might be a joke to him, but it wasn't a very funny one as far as Chris and Mike were concerned. 'She just said they'd been taken over by a bigger company,' she admitted. 'But she didn't need to give me the details. Believe me, I know what happens when smaller companies get taken over by bigger ones, and I don't suppose it's any different here.'

'Oh, I think you'll find it is,' said Jake, with that infuriating undercurrent of amusement. 'Port Lincoln is a different place from London.' He glared at her, and she could see the smile just deepening the intriguing dent at the corner of his mouth. 'Very different.'

The airport at Port Lincoln seemed to be a long way from the town. Phyllida eyed the distant glow of its lights in dismay as the little plane sank lower and lower towards a suspiciously empty-looking collection of buildings set alone in the darkness.

'Will your cousin have waited?' Jake asked as the plane taxied slowly to a halt. 'I presume she was expecting you on the eight forty-five flight?'

'No, she doesn't know I'm coming,' said Phyllida, her heart sinking as she realised that her journey wasn't over yet. She still had to get from the airport to Chris's house. 'At least, she *does* know I'm coming,' she added hurriedly as Jake opened his mouth, no doubt to make some caustic comment, 'but she doesn't know when.

'All the flights to Australia were completely full for December and January, so I had to go on a wait-list. A seat came up at the very last minute—I only just had time to pack! I did try ringing Chris, to let her know that I was on my way, but I couldn't get a reply. I didn't want to miss the flight, so in the end I just came...'

Phyllida found herself trailing to a halt, as if she were confessing to some idiocy instead of a perfectly reasonable decision. She had wanted to come, an opportunity had arisen and she had taken it. What was wrong with that?

Jake glanced at her, his brows raised. 'You just upped and left at a moment's notice? Seems a funny way to organise a sabbatical.'

'I'd made all the arrangements,' said Phyllida defensively, even as she wondered why she was bothering to explain herself to Jake Tregowan. 'It wasn't a spur-of-the-moment decision.'

Well, it *had* been originally, but in the end it had taken over three weeks before the travel agent had had enough of her badgering and had in desperation found her a wait-listed seat on a flight out of London. It had involved changing planes four times at various Asian airports, but at the time Phyllida had been so desperate to get away that she would have accepted anything.

The engine died, and the blur of the propellers slowed until she could see the individual blades turning slowly, as if exhausted by all their effort. Jake unclipped his seatbelt and climbed into the back to open the door and heave her suitcase out onto the tarmac.

Phyllida winced as she heard the loud thump, remembering how many shampoos, cleansers and moisturisers were tucked away in every available inch, pushed down shoes or wrapped in underwear. If every baggage handler since London had treated her case like Jake, she dreaded to think of what a mess there would be when she opened it.

Sighing, she retrieved her shoes from the floor by her seat and tried to put them on, but her feet were so swollen that it was an agonising squeeze. In the end she decided that she would have to go barefoot, and to hell with elegance.

Getting into the plane had been bad enough; getting out looked as if it was going to be even more daunting. Phyllida clutched her bag to her chest with one hand and held onto her shoes with the other as she peered down at Jake, who was looking up at her with an expression of irritated resignation.

'You can get out of your door onto the wing and climb down from there if you'd rather,' he said impatiently. 'But whatever you decide to do, do it quickly!'

Phyllida eyed the wing dubiously. It looked just as bad a drop as this one, and would involve yet more awkward clambering in her tight skirt. No, she would just have to jump down from here.

With an inward sigh, she dropped her bag and shoes down to Jake, and wriggled up her skirt so that she could sit down in the doorway and dangle her legs over the edge. It wasn't that big a drop, but the very thought of landing heavily on her poor feet made her flinch.

Jake muttered something under his breath and stepped forward to hold up his arms. 'I thought you were in a hurry to get to Port Lincoln?'

'I am.'

'Then will you please stop dithering around and just *jump*?'

There was no way she was going to jump, but his peremptory command was enough to get Phyllida moving. Edging forward, she eased herself off the edge, and suddenly Jake's arms were there, holding her firmly around the waist and lifting her gently to the ground.

Phyllida's hands found his shoulders, and tightened there to steady herself. She could feel the reassuring strength of his muscles through the fine cotton shirt, the hardness of his hands against her body, and then wished she hadn't noticed.

Glancing up to thank him, she found him looking down into her face with an unreadable expression, and the words dried in her throat as she was shaken by a sudden, terrifying gust of awareness. His hands seemed to be burning through her suit onto her body, and her fingers itched with the desire to slide over his shoulders, to drift down his arms and smooth along his skin, over the short dark hairs and back up to the rock-like security of his chest.

Appalled by the treacherous drift of her thoughts, Phyllida jerked herself out of his hold, passionately grateful for the darkness that hid the burning colour in her cheeks. 'I don't know why you can't get yourself a proper set of steps,' she muttered, instead of thanking him as she had originally intended.

'I can usually rely on my passengers to wear a proper set of travelling clothes,' he pointed out, unperturbed.

There was something unsettling about the way his eyes gleamed through the darkness. Phyllida was sure that he was secretly laughing at her. What if he had guessed how she had wanted to run her hands over him, to touch him and feel him? Oh, God, what if he had? She bent to pick up her bag and shoes.

'Yes, well...' She cleared her throat awkwardly, desperate to get away from his disturbing presence. 'Thank you for the lift. I appreciate it.' Tilting her case back on its wheels, she swung her bag over her shoulder, shifted her shoes to her spare hand and wished Jake a stiff goodbye.

'Where are you going?' he asked, and this time the amusement was obvious.

'I won't impose on your kindness any longer,' she said, very much on her dignity. 'I'll take a taxi to my cousin's house.'

'You'd be lucky to find a taxi out here at this time of night!' he said. 'This isn't Heathrow.'

'I'll find something,' she said, with a stubborn tilt of her chin.

Jake looked resigned. 'Still trying to prove that you can look after yourself, Phyllida?'

'I *can* look after myself!' Phyllida readjusted her grip on her suitcase with a defiant look. 'Goodbye,' she said tightly, and set off towards the terminal without waiting for him to reply.

She felt like stalking, but her bare, swollen feet ached so much that she was reduced to a less than dignified hobble. At least going so slowly meant that her case behaved with more restraint. It only fell over once. Stooping wearily to pick it up, Phyllida glanced back at the plane, irrationally piqued to discover that, far from staring after her in consternation, Jake was unconcernedly setting blocks behind the wheels.

Determined not to look back again, she carried doggedly on to the terminal building. It was certainly the
smallest airport she had ever been in, but the terminal
itself—barely bigger than her sitting-room at home—was
clean and modern—and completely empty. Phyllida
pulled open the glass door and, in spite of her best in-
tentions, glanced over her shoulder. But Jake was nowhere in sight.

Good. He was the most disagreeable, obnoxious man
she had ever met, and she was happy to think that she
would never have to see him again. Very happy.

Pushing her way through the doors leading to the front
of the terminal, she found herself in what was obviously
a pick-up area. Any taxis would certainly be waiting here,
but of course there weren't any. Jake had been right.
There were no taxis, no buses, no nothing.

She was stuck.

If Phyllida had been thinking clearly, she would have
realised that Jake would have a vehicle, that there would
be a phone somewhere she could use to ring Chris, or
call a taxi out to pick her up. But she was tired and disorientated by the long flight, and thinking clearly was
the last thing she was capable of. All she knew was that
this ghastly journey seemed as if it was never going to
end, and as she looked around her hopelessly it was impossible to imagine a time when this would all be over.

Phyllida was overwhelmed by a sudden, desperate
conviction that she was doomed to spend the rest of her
life waiting here in front of this deserted airport.

She slumped wearily down onto her suitcase. Somehow
this last blow was the worst. She hadn't cried once after
she lost her job, or after that terrible argument with
Rupert. Instead, she had let her unhappiness crystallise
into a hard, burning anger and a fierce determination
to show them all just how wrong they were. She wouldn't

have given them the satisfaction of crying then—or when everything else had leapt on the bandwagon of disaster and gone wrong too.

Her car had been broken into, the washing machine had leaked all over the kitchen floor, she had lost one of a favourite pair of earrings... Trivial problems, easily dealt with normally, but all had accumulated into a great weight on her spirits that made coping with even the most minor of crises an insuperable task.

Phyllida hadn't given in, though. She had gritted her teeth, thought of the sun and the sea in Chris's photograph, and refused to cry. She had always despised girls who burst into tears at the most minor provocation, but now, as she sat on her hated suitcase, the problem of how to get the last few miles to Port Lincoln assumed the proportions of a major disaster. Putting her hands abruptly to her face, she succumbed at last to the shamefully weak tears of exhaustion and frustration.

Behind her, the doors were pushed open and footsteps approached.

Jake.

Phyllida's face was buried in her hands, and she couldn't see anything, but the tingling of her spine told her who it was more clearly than words. She stiffened, hastily brushing the tears from her cheeks and turning her face into the shadows.

'What's the matter?' asked Jake, and Phyllida's precarious hold on her control shattered completely.

'What do you think the matter is?' she demanded furiously. 'I've just had the worst month of my life, followed by the worst journey of my life, and now I'm stuck in the middle of nowhere, when all I want to do is get to Chris's house. And you were right, there aren't any taxis, and I'll probably have to spend all night here, and

I'm tired and cold and hungry, and my feet hurt and I want to go home!'

Burying her face back into her hands, she burst into fresh tears. 'I never cry,' she wept. 'It's just that I'm tired...'

'It's hard work looking after yourself, isn't it?' said Jake.

Phyllida hated the way laughter warred with irritation in his voice. Here she was, reduced to this pitiful state, and he found it funny!

'Go away!' she sobbed, rather muffled.

There was no reply other than an exasperated sigh, and when she peeked through her fingers she saw with incredulity that he had taken her at her word and was walking away. He was just going to leave her here, she realised, aghast. How heartless could you get?

Phyllida would have died rather than run after him, but his desertion was the final straw, and the knowledge that she had sent away her one chance of help didn't help. Unable to think of anything better to do, she dropped her head into her arms and abandoned herself to her misery.

She was crying so bitterly that she didn't hear the sound of an engine starting in the car park, or even realise that it was coming towards her until the dazzle of headlights swept over her. She lifted her head to see a big four-wheel drive turn in to where she sat, a miserably huddled figure in the unforgiving light of the neon strip over her head.

A door slammed, and she squinted into the lights as Jake came striding round the bonnet towards her. 'Leave me alone!' she muttered, but surreptitiously wiped the mascara that had run down from her eyes with her knuckle.

Jake ignored her anyway, hauling her to her feet without a word and reaching down for her suitcase.

'What are you doing?'

'What do you think I'm doing?' He mimicked her earlier outburst. 'It's only fair to tell you that I too have had a long, frustrating day, topped off by having a strange woman thrust into my plane. And I do *not* feel like dealing sympathetically with hysterics at this time of night, so get in!'

'I am not hysterical!' said Phyllida, with more than a touch of hysteria. 'I'm just tired—'

'I know, and your feet hurt,' Jake interrupted her unsympathetically. 'If you stopped thinking about them, they wouldn't hurt nearly so much.'

'And if you knew how much they hurt, you wouldn't even suggest thinking about anything else,' she retorted sullenly as he threw the case into the back of the car. At least his reappearance had stopped her crying, which, as she was uncomfortably aware, had only too clearly been verging on the hysterical.

Conscious of what a mess she must be looking, she wiped at the tearstains on her cheeks with the backs of her hands and tucked her hair behind her ears.

The gesture made her look curiously vulnerable in her bare feet and her smart suit, grubby now after her struggles to get into the plane. Her brown eyes were enormous in her pale face, and the bright, vivid look that usually characterised her was muted by tiredness.

'Nothing could take my mind off my feet at the moment,' she added, lifting one so that she could inspect it gingerly and wondering if she would ever be able to walk normally again.

'You must be able to think of something that'll stop you feeling so sorry for yourself,' he said, reluctant amusement creeping back into his voice.

'You suggest something, if you're so clever,' snapped Phyllida, changing feet and grimacing at the angry red marks where her shoes had dug into her toes. 'And I'll think about it!'

'All right,' said Jake equably, and calmly took her in his arms. 'How about this?'

Phyllida, still balancing on one tender foot, was taken completely unawares and toppled against him, clutching automatically at his chest as he bent his head and kissed her.

His mouth was cool and firm, the effect of his touch electrifying. Phyllida clung to the front of his shirt, so shaken by the strange, jolting excitement that she was afraid her legs would simply give way beneath her if she let go. Jake's kiss was deliberately tantalising, deliciously persuasive, and she was quite unprepared for her own leap of response.

It was as if she had lost all control over her own body, which had succumbed with barely a protest to the enticing beat of a sudden, shocking desire that was drumming along her senses. Her mind might shriek at her to pull away, but her lips parted beneath his regardless, and her treacherous hands slid slowly down his chest and around his waist to savour the taut power of his body. He was lean and reassuringly hard, all compact strength, like tempered steel.

Phyllida had lost all sense of time and place. She had forgotten her tiredness, forgotten the fact that Jake Tregowan was to all effects and purposes a perfect stranger. All that mattered was the wash of sensation that had engulfed her the moment his mouth had touched hers, swirling her around and leaving her giddy with a new and totally unexpected pleasure.

She had no idea how long the kiss lasted—it might have been seconds, it might have been hours—and when Jake released her she could only blink up at him dazedly.

He grinned at her expression. 'How are your feet now?'

'Feet?' She stared at him blankly.

'I *thought* that might work,' said Jake with satisfaction, calmly walking over to open the passenger door for her. 'All you needed was a little distraction.'

'A...a *distraction*?' Phyllida didn't seem to be able to do anything more than echo him stupidly. She shook her head, as if to clear it, and reality hit her like a slap in the face.

Jake had kissed her in the most casual way possible, and she had responded with humiliating eagerness. She had *never* reacted like that before. What must he think of her?

Shock had made her face even paler than before, but now a rush of colour surged up her throat and stained her cheeks with embarrassment. Jake didn't seem to notice anything amiss. He was still too busy congratulating himself on the success of his tactics.

'You've got to admit that it was effective,' he said. 'I must remember it as a cure for imminent hysteria in the future.'

Phyllida opened her mouth to deny vehemently any suggestion of hysteria in her behaviour, then remembered that she could hardly claim to have been in full possession of her senses when he kissed her, and shut it again. The last thing she wanted was for Jake to think that she had known exactly what she was doing.

Phyllida chose not to remember how easily she could have pushed him away. The fact that she hadn't reacted with justifiable outrage just proved that she wasn't herself!

She should have been angry... She *was* angry, now she came to think about it. Phyllida's eyes snapped as she remembered how he had taken advantage of her, how he had captured her lips with the same casual competence with which he did everything else. And then he had dared to laugh at her!

'Are you coming?' said Jake, still holding open the door.

'I'm not getting into a car with a man who...who *grabs* me like that!'

'I was grabbing you in a good cause,' he pointed out, assuming an expression of hurt indignation that made Phyllida want to hit him. 'I was merely giving you something else to think about. It was your suggestion, after all.'

'A kiss wasn't exactly what I had in mind!'

'It worked, didn't it? You could still be grizzling about your feet, but you're complaining about me kissing you instead.'

'What do you expect me to do?' she demanded. 'Kiss your feet?'

'Well, I think you might be a little more grateful.'

'I don't feel very grateful,' said Phyllida sullenly.

'You might not be feeling grateful, but at least you're feeling better,' said Jake. 'You must be if you're refusing a lift into town. I suppose that means you're planning to walk? It's about twenty minutes in a car, so you should be there by morning.' He watched Phyllida's expression as she assimilated this.

'There isn't a lot of traffic out here at this time of night,' he went on, 'but if you're prepared to walk, that won't bother you, will it? You could set off right now...or you could stop being silly and get in the car!'

Phyllida hesitated, biting her lip, then gave in. Without looking at Jake, she climbed into the passenger seat, and

he shut the door behind her with deliberately mock
gallantry.

He drove with the same sureness and competence with
which he had flown the plane. It occurred to Phyllida
that it was odd to feel so safe with someone she knew
absolutely nothing about. She didn't know who he was,
where he lived or what he did, but somehow he didn't
feel like a stranger.

It was as if she had always known that reassuringly
capable air, the understated but unmistakable toughness,
the warm strength of his hands and the way his smile
curled the corner of that cool, firm mouth.

His mouth... Something stirred inside Phyllida as she
remembered how it had felt against hers. Something disturbing that uncurled itself and shivered up and down
her spine. His lips had been as sure as his hands, surprisingly warm, dangerously persuasive, his kiss ter-
rifyingly exciting. Phyllida began to wish she was still
thinking about her feet.

They seemed to have been driving for hours through
the darkness, along an interminably straight road. Preoccupied by her own thoughts, Phyllida had hardly
noticed her surroundings—or what there was to see of
them—but at last the lights of Port Lincoln appeared
spread out before them, curving around the bay with its
long pier jutting out from the huge grain silos and the
dark bulk of Boston Island looming in the distance.

Acutely aware that she had been less than gracious
about accepting a lift, Phyllida told Jake Chris's address
rather awkwardly. He nodded without comment, but she
was left with the peculiar conviction that he hadn't
needed to be told—a suspicion that strengthened when,
only a couple of minutes later, he drew up outside a
neat bungalow.

'Here we are—number forty-three.' He hadn't even had to look at the number, and Phyllida looked at him accusingly.

'You knew where you were going all along, didn't you?'

Jake grinned as he got out of the car and retrieved her suitcase from the back, carrying it up to the door. 'I have to admit that I've been here before,' he said unrepentantly.

'You know Chris and Mike?'

'Very well. I recognised them as soon as I saw that photograph.'

'You might have told me!' protested Phyllida.

'I might have done,' he agreed. 'But then, I thought you'd find out anyway, sooner or later.'

Phyllida regarded him angrily. 'You mean I'm likely to see you again?' It was bad enough him having kissed her, without knowing that she would have to face him again with the memory of her own response between them!

'I'm afraid so,' said Jake, with that disconcerting laugh in his voice. 'Never mind, Phyllida, at least you've arrived at last—and the light's on, so Chris is home. Aren't you going to go in?'

Phyllida's face was a study in frustration. She was longing to tell Jake exactly what she thought of his duplicity, but she could hardly do that now that she knew he was a friend of Chris. Besides, if it hadn't been for him, she wouldn't be here at all. It was all very annoying.

Jake was watching her with amusement, obviously having no trouble interpreting her expression. Phyllida took a deep breath and gathered the tattered remnants of her dignity about her.

'Yes ... Well, I'll go in, then.' She cleared her throat and held out her hand, so that he didn't get any ideas about kissing her again. 'Er, thank you for everything.'

'Everything?' he queried mockingly, taking her hand. His fingers closed around hers, and Phyllida's nerves jolted in reaction.

She snatched her hand away. 'Not quite everything,' she said coldly, knowing quite well that he was referring to that awful kiss.

Jake grinned. 'Enjoy your stay in Port Lincoln,' was all he said. He got back into his car and drove off, leaving Phyllida with a perverse sense of disappointment that he hadn't even tried to kiss her again. Her hand felt very odd, too.

She looked down at it with a peculiar expression, as if expecting it to be glowing in the dark. It felt uncomfortably sensitive, as if every line of his palm had imprinted itself on hers, and she flexed her fingers experimentally before realising how ridiculously she was behaving.

Shaking her hand irritably, to rid herself of the feeling, she took a firm grip of herself, along with her bag and shoes, pushed open the gate, and limped the last few feet to Chris's door.

CHAPTER THREE

HALF an hour later, Phyllida was curled up in an armchair with a glass of champagne in her hand. The warmth of Chris's welcome had made the whole ghastly trip worthwhile, and she smiled affectionately across at her cousin.

Chris was tall, blonde and serenely pretty, with none of Phyllida's dark, quicksilver quality. The two girls could hardly have been more different—in temperament as well as looks.

Completely lacking in vanity, Chris always wore plain, sensible clothes, while Phyllida was famous for her jazzy earrings and unsuitable shoes. Chris was an outdoor girl; Phyllida belonged in a city—rushing from gym to office, office to wine bar, wine bar to party, in a hectic whirl of activity—and yet, in spite of all the differences between them, the cousins shared a closeness that was quite unaffected by the distance that was normally between them. They might have last seen each other a week ago, instead of the five years it had been.

Phyllida was fond of Mike too, but she wasn't sorry to have Chris to herself. Mike, it appeared, had taken the car up to Queensland to see if there might be better opportunities to start a marine charter company in the Whitsunday Islands.

'It must have been awful for you,' Phyllida sympathised, when Chris told her about losing the business they had built up in Port Lincoln to a company called Sailaway.

'It could have been worse,' said Chris, cheerfully philosophical as always. 'We got a good price for our boats, and it wasn't as if we suddenly found ourselves out of a job. Mike carried on skippering inexperienced parties, and when his help took off without warning, Jake took me on in her place.'

Phyllida's heart gave a sickening lurch and her hand jerked, slopping champagne over her skirt. 'Jake?'

'Jake Tregowan. He owns Sailaway.' Chris glanced curiously at her cousin's appalled expression. 'What's the matter?'

'Nothing,' said Phyllida in a hollow voice. Oh, God, why did it have to be *him*? 'Nothing at all.'

'He's been absolutely fantastic,' Chris went on enthusiastically. 'He didn't *have* to buy us out. It would have made much more sense for him to wait for us to go bust, but he stepped in just in time before we lost everything. He didn't have to take Mike on as a skipper either. There are plenty of other experienced sailors who'd be delighted to work for him.' She smiled. 'He's got quite a reputation as a skipper himself—he's won the Sydney-Hobart twice.'

'What's that?' asked Phyllida, still frantically trying to remember what she had said to Jake about the company that had taken over Chris and Mike's business.

It was bad enough discovering that he knew them, without her having held forth about his supposedly callous treatment of them. Why, why, *why* hadn't she kept her mouth shut? Chris hadn't complained in her letter, but, still smarting from the effects of a takeover herself, she had simply assumed that Chris's experience would have been as bitter as hers. No wonder Jake had seemed amused!

He could have told her, though, Phyllida reasoned resentfully. Instead he had chosen to let her make a fool of herself, knowing that she would be bound to find out the truth from Chris.

Her cousin was still talking about the Sydney-Hobart. 'It's one of the toughest ocean races in the world. The conditions on the Bass Strait can be horrific. I love sailing, but you wouldn't catch me out there! Jake seems to love it, though. He's a real yachtsman—only really at home on a boat.

'You'd never guess he came from such a wealthy background,' she went on confidentially. 'Tregowan's is one of the biggest companies in New South Wales. Jake even ran it for a while, but he opted out of the rat race and now he just keeps an eye on their interests in Adelaide. He says he doesn't want to waste his life sitting behind a desk when he could be on a boat.'

Well, that explained the private plane and the intangible aura of wealth and confidence, Phyllida thought, still chagrined. But how was she to have guessed that he ran a marine charter company when he dressed like the successful executive he had obviously once been?

'He sounds quite a paragon,' she said lightly. She longed to ask more, but she didn't want Chris to wonder why she was showing such interest in a man she had never met.

Her cousin had exclaimed at the state of her suit, and demanded to know how she had managed to appear out of nowhere, but, with her hand still tingling from his touch, Phyllida had given a vague answer, curiously reluctant to talk about Jake. Now it seemed too late to explain.

'Oh, he is!' said Chris cheerfully. 'If I didn't love Mike so much, I'm sure I'd be in love with Jake! And, talking of love, what's happened to this Rupert you wrote to me about? I thought you were engaged? Couldn't he come with you?'

'He wasn't invited,' said Phyllida with a wry smile.

'Oh, dear. What happened? All you said on the phone was that you were planning to come out for three months and would get a flight as soon as possible.'

'I didn't tell you that I was sacked?'

'No!' Chris sat bolt-upright and stared at Phyllida. 'I don't believe it! You loved that job!'

'I know, but Pritchard Price was only a small agency, and when Liedermann, Marshall & Jones took it over they decided that a mere woman couldn't be a group account director. They gave my job to one of their own executives—male, of course!

'The fact that I'd been a very successful group account director for the last two years didn't count, apparently,' she remembered bitterly. 'They said it was all part of the reorganisation involved in merging two agencies, but if I'd been a man there would have been no question about keeping me on.'

Chris frowned. She knew how much her job had meant to Phyllida. 'Rupert doesn't work for the firm that sacked you, does he?'

'Rupert? No, he's a wine merchant. Very successful, but very traditional—old school tie, and that kind of thing. That should have been a warning,' Phyllida added bleakly.

'Why, what did he do?'

'I was so angry when I heard about my job that I stormed round to see Rupert. I thought he understood how much I cared about my work, but he had the nerve to tell me that he thought it would all work out for the best!' Phyllida's face was flushed with the memory of her blazing indignation at Rupert's patronising reaction.

'We hadn't been engaged very long, and we hadn't really talked about when the wedding would be or what would happen after we were married. I'd assumed that things would go on as before, but it turned out that Rupert thought that wives should be kept firmly at home. Losing my job meant that I could give up my "career nonsense" and settle down to looking after him!'

She shook her head, still outraged whenever she thought about Rupert's attitude. 'I can see now that we just didn't know each other well enough to get married, and that it would have been a disaster if we had, but at the time it all blew up into the most terrible argument.' Her careful smile went a little awry. 'I ended up throwing his ring in his face and walking out.'

'Oh, Phyl, I'm so sorry,' said Chris sympathetically. 'Two blows in one day!'

'The awful thing is that when I'd calmed down a bit, I realised that losing my job hurt far more than losing Rupert,' Phyllida confessed. 'Oh, I know I thought he was perfect—handsome, successful, sophisticated—but I couldn't marry anyone who thought of me as just another decorative item.'

'He sounded ideal for you,' sighed Chris. 'But then, perhaps you're like me, and need someone completely different?'

For some reason, Jake Tregowan's image wavered in front of Phyllida's eyes.

She could picture him far too clearly for her own comfort: the cool, distinctive angles of his face, the decisive line of his jaw, the quiet, curling mouth and those disconcerting eyes with their smile lurking behind the exasperated expression ...

They were all unaccountably familiar, and she frowned. 'All I need at the moment is to get away from it all for a bit.'

'Well, you've come to the right place for that,' said Chris cheerfully. 'Unfortunately this is a very busy time at the marina, so I'll have to work, but you can come along too if you like. It's hard work, but fun—and you'll like Jake.'

Now, if ever, was the time to tell Chris that she had already met Jake, and hadn't liked him at all, but the words stuck in Phyllida's throat. For some reason, Chris obviously thought that he was wonderful, and Phyllida didn't want to spoil their first evening by disillusioning her. The complicated explanations could wait until tomorrow.

But Phyllida never had the chance to explain just why she had unaccountably forgotten to mention her meeting with Jake Tregowan. She fell into an exhausted sleep as soon as her head hit the pillow, and didn't wake until the sun came streaming into her room.

A phone was ringing somewhere. That must have been what had woken her, she realised, but it stopped abruptly when the receiver was picked up. Chris must still be at home.

Phyllida lay for a while trying to remember the last time she had seen hot, bright sunshine, but her thoughts began to drift to the previous night. In the clear light of day, the trip from Adelaide had acquired an even more surreal quality in retrospect. Had she really flown through the darkness in that tiny plane? Had that been *her* sobbing on her suitcase? Had Jake Tregowan really kissed her, and had she really kissed him back?

Phyllida sat up abruptly. It would have been nice to dismiss it all as a bad dream, but Jake's memory was much too vivid for that. Her palm still tingled where he had clasped her hand. He was real, all right. Much too real.

Swinging her legs out of bed, she pulled on a towelling dressing-gown rather crossly. She would have liked to have stayed in bed, but Jake Tregowan had ruined that.

She had no intention of lying there thinking about *him*. Now that she was awake, she might as well get up.

Yawning, she tied the robe round her as she wandered along to the kitchen. Chris was there, talking on the phone with her back to the door, but as Phyllida hesitated in the doorway she put down the receiver and turned.

The look on her face drove all thoughts of Jake Tregowan from Phyllida's mind. 'Chris! What on earth's the matter? You look terrible!'

'It's Mike,' said Chris, her expression blank with shock. 'That was the hospital in Brisbane. He's been in an accident. Oh, Phyl, what am I going to do?'

Phyllida paid off the taxi and turned to look at the marina. In front of her steps led down to a long jetty, branching out into wooden pontoons which were lined with an impressive array of yachts. They rocked gently in the swell, their masts tall and straight against the vast, glaring blueness of the sky and their pennants slapping in the breeze that sighed and sang through the rigging.

At the end of the jetty was a small wooden building. Phyllida could see the sign painted over its door: SAILAWAY. She swallowed, and wiped her hands surreptitiously on her trousers. It had all sounded so easy when she had assured Chris that she would sort everything out with Jake Tregowan, but the prospect of seeing him again made her heart thud painfully against her ribs.

Phyllida squared her shoulders. This was ridiculous! She had coped with far more difficult situations, soothed angry clients and sorted out seemingly intractable problems, so she ought to be more than capable of dealing with Jake Tregowan. She had promised Chris.

A tiny frown creased her forehead. Chris—sturdy, reliable Chris—had gone to pieces when she had heard about Mike's accident, and it had been Phyllida who had arranged a flight to Brisbane, organised a taxi and packed a case. And now she was here to keep the promise she had made as she hugged her goodbye at the airport.

Taking a deep breath, Phyllida walked down the steps and along the jetty to the Sailaway office. The door was standing open to the sunlight. It was stupid to be so nervous, she told herself as she hesitated outside. She had been in such a confused state last night that she had probably built Jake up out of all proportion. She told herself that in the clear light of day he would turn out to be a perfectly ordinary, inoffensive man.

But when she stepped through the door and saw Jake standing by a filing cabinet she knew that she hadn't imagined any of it. He had turned as she knocked lightly on the door, and his brows shot up in surprise.

He was dressed very casually today, in jeans and a plain white T-shirt, but if anything he looked even tougher and more assured than she remembered—the planes of his face more distinct, the impression of controlled competence more striking than ever. His eyes seemed greener, too, flecked with grey, but just as unnervingly sharp as they had been last night.

He dropped the file he had been holding onto the top of the cabinet and pushed the drawer shut with the flat of his hand. 'Well, well,' he said. 'What an unexpected surprise! Don't tell me you need another lift somewhere?'

'No.' It wasn't fair the way the air whooshed from her lungs whenever she saw him, leaving her breathless and flustered. She was supposed to be the cool, capable career girl, not the dithering idiot she became as soon as Jake looked at her with those unsettling, ironic eyes of his. She cleared her throat. 'I came to talk to you.'

'I'm flattered.' He swept a pile of brochures off a chair and gestured her towards it with what Phyllida was sure was mock courtesy. 'You'd better sit down.'

Unsure of where to begin, Phyllida looked around her. Windows on three sides gave a good view of the marina, and through a door at the back she could see a storeroom stacked with piles of towels, linen and cleaning materials. A marine radio stood on the desk, crackling out a weather report, and Jake leant across to turn it down.

'I suppose Chris told you where to find me,' he said, swinging the desk chair round and sitting down. 'I wasn't expecting to see you so soon. When I left you last night, I was under the distinct impression that you'd be happy if you never saw me again!'

Faint colour tinged her cheeks as she remembered how flustered and ungracious she had been. 'That was last night,' she said. 'I'm here for Chris, not for myself. She's had to go to Brisbane. Mike's had an accident.'

His face changed to instant concern. 'That's terrible news,' he said, shocked. 'Is he badly hurt?'

'We don't really know yet. When the hospital rang this morning, they said he hadn't regained consciousness.'

Jake frowned. 'Do they know what happened?'

'He was driving down to Brisbane on his way home,' said Phyllida. 'A witness told the police that he swerved to avoid an overtaking truck and his car turned over as it went off the road.' Her voice wavered slightly and she drew a steadying breath. 'Poor Chris was in a terrible state. I put her on a flight up to Brisbane about an hour ago. She's going to ring me tonight and let me know how he is.'

'Is there anything I can do?' asked Jake, getting to his feet and pacing the office as he assimilated the news.

'Yes,' said Phyllida evenly, glad that he had given her an opening. 'There is. You can take me on in Chris's place while she's away.'

He swung round. '*What*?'

'Chris is worried about her job,' she explained hastily. The last thing she wanted was for Jake to think that *she* wanted to come and work for him! 'With Mike out of action, that's the only income they've got, and she's afraid that if she has to be away for a while, you might have to give her job to someone else. Apparently this is your busiest time?'

'It is, but there's no question of Chris losing her job,' said Jake angrily. 'Quite apart from my responsibilities as an employer, I wouldn't do that to Chris.' He glowered accusingly at Phyllida. 'She and Mike are friends of mine.'

'There's no need to bite my head off!' she snapped. 'It wasn't *my* idea. I told Chris you'd have to be a monster to treat her like that, but she wasn't thinking rationally. She was in such a panic about Mike that she couldn't deal calmly with anything. When something like that happens, you lose all sense of proportion. Trivial things suddenly become major disasters...'

Phyllida faltered as she felt Jake's sardonic eyes on her. She knew he was remembering how she had sat and wept on her suitcase last night, and she shifted uncomfortably in her seat. How trivial her problems had been compared to Chris's!

'Chris was frantic,' she went on, trying to sound calm and reasonable, and not at all like a girl who would burst into tears just because she was tired and her feet hurt. 'She was desperate to go to Mike, but she was worried about letting you down.

'I wanted to go with her to Brisbane, but in the end the only way I could reassure her was to offer to work for you in her place. She said that way she'd know that she could come back whenever she was ready, without letting anybody else get their hopes up about it turning into a permanent job.'

Jake put his hands in his pockets and stood frowning out of the window. A motor boat cruised past, leaving the moored yachts rocking in its curved wake.

'You'll just have to reassure Chris that there's no need for her to worry. I'll have to get someone else in to help out over the next few weeks, but it'll only be a temporary measure, and I'll carry on paying her as normal so that money isn't a problem. She can have her job back whenever she wants it—and Mike too, of course. Though if he's badly hurt it may be some time before he's fit to sail again.'

Phyllida twisted round in her seat to watch him. 'You don't want me to come and work for you, do you?'

'Frankly, no. I'd much rather get someone more suitable in.'

'What do you mean, "more suitable"?' she asked, offended. 'What's wrong with me?'

'You're English, for a start.'

'What difference does that make?'

Jake turned from the window and came back to his seat. 'I took on an English girl for the summer last November. She seemed to have all the right experience, and I thought I'd give international relations a chance, but she was a sloppy worker and she only lasted a couple of weeks before deciding that it was too much like hard work and heading off to Adelaide. If it hadn't been for Chris, I would have been stuck. English girls aren't top of my popularity list at the moment.'

'So?' said Phyllida defiantly. 'I'm not asking you to like me.'

'It's just as well,' said Jake, with a distinct edge to his voice, and they glared at each other. He sighed abruptly. 'I wonder if you realise quite what's involved?'

'Chris didn't have time to tell me much, but I gathered it was some cooking and a bit of cleaning.'

'It's rather more than that,' said Jake, raking his fingers through his hair in exasperation. 'I operate fifteen boats from here. Some are chartered by experienced sailors, other parties need a skipper like Mike to go with them. Occasionally a party will bring everything with them, but most people ask us to do the provisioning for them.

'It's very flexible. They can either take the food we've provided and do the cooking themselves, or Chris prepares as many meals as possible in advance so they just need to be heated up.' He swivelled round to face Phyllida again. 'Can you cook?'

'Of course,' she said loftily. 'My dinner parties are famous.'

'I'm talking about good, plain food, not pretentious dinner party fare,' said Jake with a repressive look. 'Sailing parties aren't interested in nouvelle cuisine.'

'Well, I expect I can manage to cook something boring, if that's what you really want!' snapped Phyllida, provoked. 'It can't be that difficult.'

'You'd be surprised,' he warned her. 'Chris not only plans the menus for each boat, but does the shopping, stocks the fridge and the lockers and prepares meals for those who've ordered them. On top of that she cleans the boats as they come in, so they're ready for the changeover. That means changing the linen in the cabins, checking the inventory and replacing anything not up to standard. Everything has to be spotless. She also helps out in the office—answering the phone, typing, that kind of thing.'

'That's not a job, that's slave labour!' said Phyllida, appalled.

'I didn't think you'd like it,' said Jake. 'Chris makes it look easy, but you're not used to working.'

'Yes, I am!' When she *thought* of the hours she'd spent in the office, working late over a report or a special presentation! Phyllida's brown eyes snapped. 'It may interest you to know that I'm used to working extremely hard!'

'You're used to sitting behind a desk and being clever,' he said, unimpressed. 'That's not work. I need someone who's not afraid to roll up her sleeves and get her hands dirty—not someone with a fancy title whose greatest physical exertion is picking up the phone!'

'I may not get my hands dirty, but I still need to be tough to survive,' Phyllida pointed out. 'I have to be able to manage people, take responsibility, and organise work so that it gets done in the most efficient way possible. Instead of sneering, you could be thinking about how to make the most of my executive skills.'

'You don't need to be able to run a committee meeting or dictate memos to clean a boat!' Jake leant forward suddenly and took her hands, turning them up to run his thumbs over her palms. 'Look at these hands! They're not tough enough to cope with weeks on end of scrubbing and polishing and scouring.'

Phyllida's mouth was dry. It was as if her whole body was focused on the light stroke of his thumbs. She was excruciatingly aware of every millimetre of his skin touching hers as the fire flickered up from palm to wrist, wrist to shoulder, and on to burn right through her, melting her bones and setting her spine aquiver.

'They'll get used to it.' Her tongue felt thick and unwieldy, and it was a real effort to get the words out.

'Ah, but will you?' Jake released her hands and sat back in his chair, studying her as if she was a rather

awkward bit of furniture he had to decide what to do
with.

'I'm tougher than I look.' She was sitting bolt-upright,
chin lifted stubbornly, although the brown eyes were wide
and indignant.

Conscious of the ridiculously pathetic impression she
must have made last night, she had made an effort to
look crisp and practical, in blue and white striped
trousers and a white top, but she was convinced that
Jake still saw her as she had been then, weeping on her
suitcase in her crumpled suit.

The light through the window caught the nut-coloured
tints in the shining bob that framed her small, determined face, and, unsettled by his inspection, she lifted
a hand and smoothed the hair behind one ear in an unconsciously nervous gesture.

'I don't think you're nearly as tough as you'd like to
think you are,' sighed Jake, and her face flamed at the
challenge.

'Try me!'

An irritable expression crossed his face. 'Last night
you were full of what a high-powered executive you were
and how important your career was. Are you really
asking me to believe you'd be happy chopping onions
and scrubbing decks for the next few weeks?'

'I would if it put Chris's mind at rest,' said Phyllida,
looking him straight in the eye. 'Look, I don't *want* to
spend my time in Australia working for you, any more
than you want to have me, but I promised Chris that I
would, so that's what I'm going to do.

'I don't know why you're objecting,' she went on
crossly. 'You said you wanted to help Chris, and this
would reassure her more than anything. Hasn't she got
enough problems at the moment without worrying about
what's happening here? Maybe I'm not the most suitable

person you could have, but I'm saving you the trouble of finding someone else, and you might at least give me a chance before you decide that I can't cope!'

She stuck her chin up proudly and stared at him with bright, challenging eyes. 'You never know, you might even find that I'm tougher than you think!'

There was a tiny silence. Jake looked at her curiously, the grey-green eyes narrowed, a gleam of what might have been admiration in their depths. 'I might,' he agreed slowly, and the air was suddenly strumming with tension. It was as if someone had flicked a switch, sending an electric charge between them, and Phyllida's heart began a slow, painful thud.

'Why are you doing this, Phyllida?' he asked. 'You don't have to. I could get someone else in and we could just tell Chris that you were working here. She wouldn't be any the wiser.'

She shook her head. 'I couldn't lie to Chris.'

'And what about your holiday?' He clicked his fingers in mock apology. 'Sorry! Your *sabbatical*. Aren't you supposed to be spending the next few weeks planning your next career moves and preparing for your great promotion?'

Phyllida's eyes slid from his. She had forgotten about that particular lie. If Jake hadn't been so sarcastic about the whole idea of her having a career, she might have been tempted to tell him the truth. As it was, she was damned if she would give him the satisfaction!

'I came out to get a change of perspective,' she said. 'All I really need is time to think, and I presume I'll be allowed to do that while I'm scrubbing the decks. Or is that too executive for you?' she added acidly.

'No, thinking's allowed,' said Jake with some amusement. 'Arguing isn't. You can leave your career at home every day. I don't want to hear about how important you are, or how different things could be if only I wasn't so unreasonable and prejudiced. A lot of the work is boring and menial, so don't say you weren't warned and don't complain!'

'You mean you'll take me on?' said Phyllida, sitting up, and he sighed.

'Only for Chris's sake. If it means so much to her, then I'm prepared to put up with you. But only if you're prepared to work as hard as she does.'

'I will,' she promised eagerly. She had begun to think that he was going to refuse to take her after all, and now she was too relieved at being able to reassure Chris to object to his tone.

'Let's hope it's not for too long,' said Jake, resigned to his fate. 'When Chris and Mike come back I'm sure we'll both welcome them with open arms, but until then it looks as if we're stuck with each other!'

CHAPTER FOUR

DECISION made, Jake immediately became brisk and businesslike. 'Have you got a driving licence?'

'Not with me,' said Phyllida guiltily. 'Packing was such a rush when a seat came up at the last minute. I never even thought about my driving licence.'

'Judging by the size of that case, you seemed to have had time to think about bringing everything else,' he commented with some acidity. 'I'd have thought a high-powered executive like you would have been a little more organised about everything.'

'I remembered everything else,' she said, stung. 'How was I to know I'd need a driving licence?'

'I suppose you were expecting Chris and Mike to act as unpaid chauffeurs?'

Phyllida ground her teeth. 'I didn't know *what* to expect! I certainly didn't expect to be cross-examined just because I forgot one piece of paper! What does it matter anyway?'

'I was going to give you the van so that you could go shopping, but now it looks as if I'm going to have to ferry you around everywhere. It's beginning to become something of a habit!'

'Well, it's not one of my choosing, I can assure you!'

'Oh, I forgot—you're the girl who's so good at looking after yourself, aren't you?' said Jake nastily. 'Funny how it always seems to involve someone else doing all the work!'

'We're only talking about the occasional trip to the shops,' Phyllida snapped. 'If it's such an appalling prospect for you, I'll find some other way to get there!'

'Like you did last night?'

'Last night was different,' she said sullenly. 'I wasn't myself, and you know it! Anybody would have given up after the journey I'd had—and you didn't help, being so...so...'

'So what?' he asked, amusement gleaming suddenly in his eyes.

'So disagreeable!' said Phyllida, provoked into an undiplomatic retort.

Jake wasn't going to let her get away with that. 'Disagreeable?' he echoed in mock astonishment. 'I carried your case, I flew you all the way to Port Lincoln, I drove you to Chris's door... What did I do that was so disagreeable?'

Phyllida felt as if she was being driven into a corner, and searched her mind frantically for some instance of his ungallant behaviour. It wasn't so much what he had done, it was the mockery in his eyes and the ironic note in his voice and the disturbing way he had made her feel, but she couldn't tell him that.

'You kissed me,' she said sulkily at last. It was the only thing she could think of that she could reasonably hold against him.

'You didn't think it was that disagreeable at the time,' said Jake unfairly, not in the least put out at being reminded of the embarrassing incident.

'You took advantage of me,' she accused him, but he only looked back at her blandly.

'In that case we're quits, aren't we?'

It was Phyllida who dropped her eyes first. Why had she brought up that wretched kiss? Its memory seemed to shimmer in the air between them, tingling on her lips and shivering down her spine. She could still feel the hardness of his body beneath her hands, the jolting excitement of his mouth on hers.

'There must be some way I can get myself around, anyway,' she said, struggling to bring the conversation back to less dangerous ground. 'Aren't there any buses?'

'This isn't London,' said Jake. 'You might be able to get to the shops all right, but even if you did you wouldn't be able to carry everything back.'

'I could get a taxi,' she said defiantly.

'You could,' he agreed, 'if you were prepared to pay for it. Because I'm not going to when I've got a perfectly good van standing empty! Were you proposing to get a taxi from Chris and Mike's house every morning, too?'

'I hadn't thought about it.'

'Well, think about it now. The marina's a long way from their house, and you certainly won't find a convenient bus waiting at the end of the road.'

Phyllida pressed her lips together. 'I've managed to hold down a tough job and live on my own in London for several years,' she reminded him coldly. 'I expect I'll be able to survive in Port Lincoln.'

'That's a matter of opinion,' said Jake astringently. He pointed out of the window. 'I live on that headland on the other side of the marina. It's close enough for you to walk if necessary.' He sounded unflatteringly resigned. 'You'd better come and stay with me, I suppose.'

'Stay with *you*?' echoed Phyllida, horrified. 'I'd rather sleep on the beach!'

Jake clicked his tongue in exasperation. 'However you got to the top of your supposedly high-flying career, it obviously wasn't by tact!'

'And you didn't get where you are by charm!' she snapped back. 'It wasn't exactly the warmest of invitations! Anyway, there's no question of my moving in with you!'

'This isn't some ruse to get my hands on your body, if that's what you're worried about, so there's really no need to react like some outraged spinster,' sighed Jake. 'Quite frankly, I can think of more congenial companions myself. I don't particularly fancy spending the next few weeks with a little spitfire, but I don't see any alternative.'

'The alternative is that I stay at Chris and Mike's house!'

'And how are you going to get here every morning?'

'I'll think of something!'

'The house is quite big enough for two of us, you know. You could treat it just like a flat.'

'I'd rather stay where I am,' said Phyllida firmly. The thought of spending her days near Jake was disturbing enough, but living with him as well...! She felt twitchy at the very idea.

Jake regarded the small, stubborn figure sitting opposite him with frustration. 'Why do you always insist on learning things the hard way, Phyllida?'

'Why do *you* refuse to accept that I can look after myself?' she retorted, and held up a hand before he could answer. 'And if you mention last night again, I shall scream! I *know* I was pathetic, but believe me, it won't happen again.' She met his sceptical gaze defiantly. 'I'm good at what I do, and I'll be good at this too. You just wait and see!'

'Well, if you're so determined to prove yourself, you can begin right now,' said Jake, resigned. He got to his feet. 'I'll show you round, then you can get straight to work. We've got a lot to do this week.'

He showed her the storeroom and the filing system, and explained how the radio worked. 'We keep a twenty-four-hour listening watch for our boats,' he said. 'So if you hear someone calling up and I'm not around, you'll have to come and answer. It should be mostly straightforward, but you may be asked for some advice. Have you got any experience of sailing?'

'Does a day-trip to Boulogne count?'

Jake sighed. 'Oh, that's a great help! You must have done *some* sailing?'

'I don't see why,' Phyllida objected. 'Sailing at home always sounds cold and wet and uncomfortable. Chris and Mike love that sort of thing, but my idea of outdoor activity is sitting on a terrace in the sun!'

Jake glanced down at her vivid face. 'You're not very like Chris, are you?'

Phyllida's expression softened. 'No, it's hard to believe that we're related, isn't it? I think we get on so well just because we *are* so different. I wish I could be more like Chris sometimes,' she admitted, wondering how best she could describe her cousin. 'She's so... restful.'

'It's certainly not a word I'd use to describe *you*,' Jake agreed, and she met his eyes challengingly.

'Oh? What *would* you use?'

He grinned unexpectedly. 'That would be telling.'

His smile took Phyllida unawares. Just when she had decided that he was even more insufferable than she had remembered, he had to go and do that to her! It had been disturbing enough in the dim light of the plane, but now her heart missed a beat.

She could see the way laughter starred lines beneath his eyes, and creased his cheeks with humour. His teeth were heartstoppingly white against his brown skin. Phyllida felt something twist alarmingly inside her. She even forgot to breathe until the sharpening look in Jake's eyes reminded her of where she was and what she was supposed to be doing.

Breathe in, breathe out. It was easy when you tried.

Outside, the sky was a blazing blue, the sun high and glaring. Phyllida had to screw up her eyes as Jake led her out to the boats. A stiff breeze from the sea blew her neat, shining brown hair about her face, and she had to hold it back with one hand as she looked down the jetty, Jake's smile still burning at the back of her mind.

The water looked almost colourless in the fierce glitter of the sun, but Phyllida could hear it slapping against the sides of the jetty and effortlessly lifting the boats up and down. She watched their gently hypnotic rise and fall as if she had never seen a yacht before, never noticed how the curve of the hull contrasted with the lance-like straightness of the mast and the geometric lines of the rigging.

It must be something to do with the diamond-bright air, she decided, so unlike the soft light of England. Everything seemed almost unnaturally distinct, every boat uniquely outlined against its neighbour. Each one was different—graceful yachts were moored next to huge motor cruisers bristling with antennae, sleek speedboats next to sturdy fishing smacks—but as they rocked together in the water it seemed to Phyllida that they all evoked the same tantalising promise of the sea, with its exhilarating freedom and freshness.

Closing her eyes, she turned her face up to the sun and sniffed at the sharp tang of the sea carried in by the breeze, smiling at the sound of the gulls squabbling on the water, the creak of the ropes and the chink and rattle of the halyards against a hundred masts.

It was all very different from the sounds she was used to: phones ringing, the chatter of computer printers, voices raised in argument or laughter, the subdued roar of traffic outside the window and the distant wail of a siren. The sounds of the marina were at once alien and strangely familiar.

In spite of everything, Phyllida was suddenly, fiercely glad that she had come, and as she opened her eyes and turned to Jake she was still smiling.

He was watching her with an odd expression in his eyes. 'I thought you'd fallen asleep,' he said, as if making an effort to sound his usual acid self.

Phyllida shook her head, and her mock-diamond earrings, shaped in a square like a battery of floodlights, flashed in the sunlight. 'I was just...thinking.'

'That makes a change, anyway,' said Jake drily, turning away to lead her along the jetty. The pontoon rose and fell beneath their feet as he told her the names of the boats, pointing out each one affectionately.

'Most of the boats are out at the moment, but this is *Persephone*. That's *Dora Dee* next to her—she's a beauty, isn't she?—and this one here is *Calypso*. She only came in yesterday, so she needs cleaning. So does *Valli*.' He pointed to a boat tied up to *Calypso*, her name proudly proclaimed on the blue cover tied neatly over the folded mainsail.

The name sounded familiar to Phyllida. 'That's one of Chris and Mike's boats, isn't it?'

'She was, until I so callously bought her from them in my ruthless takeover of their company.'

Phyllida had the grace to blush. 'I'm sorry about that,' she said awkwardly, cringing as she remembered how she had held forth about her cousin's misfortune. 'Chris told me what really happened. She's very grateful to you.

I just jumped to the wrong conclusions from her letter—takeovers were rather a sore point with me at the time.'

'Does that mean that you've now jumped to the right conclusions about me?' Jake asked.

There was a teasing look in his grey-green eyes, and the long, cool mouth twitched as he tried not to smile at her determinedly humble expression. His hands were thrust casually into the pockets of his jeans, and the wind riffled his brown hair, fluttering the cotton T-shirt against the hard outline of his body.

For one dismaying moment, Phyllida felt her insides melt as she looked at him. It wasn't fair the way he could do that to her just by standing there, with his eyes half screwed up against the bright light and the smile tugging at his mouth. Resentment made her sound colder than she had intended. 'I think I'll suspend judgement on that until I know you better.'

'It's not like you to be so cautious, is it, Phyllida?'

'How do you know what I'm like?' she demanded suspiciously, following him on down the jetty.

'Observation,' said Jake. He stepped from the pontoon into the cockpit of a boat with *Ariadne* painted on her side and held out a hand to help Phyllida across. 'You told me yourself that you were impulsive, and everything I've seen of you so far suggests that you're far too prone to leap before you look!'

Dithering on the edge of the pontoon, Phyllida came to the reluctant conclusion that, unless she accepted his hand, there was no way to get down into the boat without making a complete and utter fool of herself. Grudgingly, she gave him her hand and let him steady her as she clambered awkwardly over the guard rails. A sudden gust of wind made the boat rock abruptly, sending her staggering against the rock-steady hardness of his body.

Cheeks aflame, she jerked herself away, only to stumble over some ropes lying coiled in the cockpit. 'It's a constant surprise to me how someone who looks so fragile and delicate can be so clumsy,' said Jake acidly, picking her up.

'I am not clumsy! Anyone would trip over with all these stupid ropes lying around!'

'I didn't notice any ropes around when you were dealing with your suitcase last night,' said Jake unfairly. 'And, for the record, these are not ropes. They're known as sheets on a boat.'

'They look like ropes to me,' Phyllida muttered under her breath, but she followed Jake down some wooden steps into a surprisingly light and airy saloon, high enough for Jake to stand up with ease. There were two comfortably padded seats on either side of a table, and a neat area with a small oven set on gimbals and a lid with a metal handle set into the worktop.

Phyllida lifted it and peered down into a sloping compartment with an element fixed to one side. 'What's this?'

'A battery-operated fridge,' said Jake. 'We put in a block of ice as well, and it'll keep food fresh for a week. You'll need to bear that in mind when drawing up your menus.'

'This is the kitchen, then?' said Phyllida, looking about her with interest, and sliding open locker doors to reveal neatly stacked plates and glasses.

'No, it's the galley,' he said repressively, and she rolled her eyes.

'Oh, all right—the *galley*.'

She was soon lost in a welter of nautical terminology as Jake showed her over the boat. She peered into the three immaculately fitted out cabins and the tiny cramped space allotted for a shower, basin and loo—or head, as she was supposed to call it now. Jake's face was alight with enthusiasm, and he ran his hand lovingly over the wooden fittings, pointing out radios, charts and compasses and a baffling array of instruments that Phyllida could only stare at blankly, until Jake accused her of not paying attention.

'I am,' she protested. 'It's just all a bit confusing if you've never been on a boat before.' She didn't tell him that it would have been a lot easier to concentrate if she hadn't kept bumping into him. There wasn't all that much room to move below deck, and whenever she stepped back from looking at something she would find herself brushing against Jake.

She was disturbingly aware of the taut solidity of his body and the feel of his steadying hand, and, infuriatingly, she kept remembering last night's kiss in vivid detail—how he had held her against him, how tantalisingly persuasive his lips had been, how the treacherous excitement had shivered along her senses. That was all far, far more confusing than bilge pumps, depth sounders or dials showing wind speed in knots.

She was immensely relieved when Jake made his way back on deck. 'Well, what do you think?' he asked, patting the fibreglass with unashamed affection.

Phyllida looked at the fibreglass and wondered if *it* tingled when he touched it. 'I think you obviously like boats more than women,' she said a little tartly. 'It's interesting that all yours have girls' names.'

'Nothing unusual in that,' said Jake with a glimmering smile. 'But since you mention it, Phyllida, you're quite right. I *do* prefer boats to women. They're just as expensive to run, but no woman ever gave the pleasure of being out at sea, with the boat singing through the waves, just you and the boat and the elements, and nobody there to nag or argue or demand to be taken home as soon as the wind gets stiff enough to mess up her hair!'

His tone was suddenly acid, and Phyllida couldn't help wondering if he was remembering anyone in particular. She wondered what it would be like to be the girl Jake loved, the girl he took sailing. It was hard to imagine the kind of girl who would worry about her hair when she had Jake.

'So there's no room for women in your life?' she asked as he helped her back onto the pontoon.

Jake glanced down at her, the grey-flecked eyes unreadable. 'I didn't say that.'

'But you haven't yet met anyone who can compete with a good sail?' Phyllida had meant to sound sarcastic, but instead succeeded in merely sounding rather put out as she pointedly drew her hand from his.

He considered her, his gaze resting on her vivid elfin face, with the wide brown eyes catching the sunlight and the hair which had been so smooth and neat tangling in the breeze. She looked small and vibrant, and somehow defiant.

'Not yet,' he said slowly.

Phyllida felt herself grow incalculably hot as his eyes slid down the line of her throat to her open collar, and on over the slender, deceptively delicate figure. 'Do you have a boat of your own, or do you charter them all?' she asked quickly.

'No, that's mine, moored at the end there.' Jake's tone changed as he pointed to a particularly elegant yacht with a gleaming wooden deck, its brass fittings glittering in the sun. 'The *Ali B*. Isn't she beautiful?'

'Gorgeous,' said Phyllida, but there was a suspicious undercurrent of jealousy to her sarcasm.

Jake laughed, unperturbed. 'I think so, anyway. Do you want to see her?'

'I thought I was here to work?' said Phyllida, who had no desire to see Jake drooling over a stupid boat. 'What shall I do first?' she asked, looking around.

'You can start by cleaning *Calypso*,' Jake told her. He took her back to the office and found her an aluminium bucket stuffed full of cleaning materials. 'You'll find water at points along the jetty,' he said, handing it to her.

Phyllida took the bucket, inspecting its contents rather dubiously. 'Is that it?' she asked as he turned back to his desk without further instructions.

'What more do you want?'

'Well...aren't you going to tell me what I should do?'

'You're the great career woman, Phyllida. Use those much-vaunted executive skills of yours to work it out for yourself. You seemed very sure you could do the job just as well as anyone else; now's your chance to prove it. I'll check things over when you've finished, and let you know if you're up to standard.'

The idea of her work being checked by Jake Tregowan brought Phyllida's chin up. So he was waiting for her to make a mess of things, was he? She would show him!

Marching down the jetty, she encountered her first problem—getting onto *Calypso* by herself. It wasn't that it was such a big jump, but the boat kept riding up and away from the pontoon, just as Phyllida was about to step off, and when she did finally manage to get one leg over the guard rail another wave caught her spreadeagled between boat and pontoon, and only an extremely undignified scramble got her onto the deck with her bucket in one piece. Phyllida brushed herself down and hoped that no one had been watching.

'Would you like me to get some water for you, Phyllida?' Jake's voice from the pontoon behind her made her swing around. 'You seemed to be having a little trouble getting aboard there.'

Of course, he *would* have been watching! Phyllida glared at him, about to tell him what he could do with his water when it occurred to her that it would be even more difficult making the jump with a full bucket of water. 'Thank you,' she said in a frosty voice, emptying the contents of the bucket onto the cockpit seat and swinging it back across the gap.

'I'm sure a professional like you will be able to master the tricky business of getting on and off a boat in no time,' said Jake with a mocking smile as he passed the full bucket back to her.

Some of the water slopped out of the bucket, and Phyllida was sorely tempted to chuck the rest of it back into Jake Tregowan's smugly smiling face. She contented herself with a freezing look and an implacable determination to clean the boat to such a pitch of perfection that even Jake wouldn't be able to find fault with it.

It proved to be much harder work than she had anticipated. The sun beat down on the fibreglass above her head, and without the cooling breeze Phyllida was soon very hot. Her shirt and trousers were sticking to her uncomfortably, and she could feel the sweat trickling down her back.

Calypso was showing all the signs of having been lived in by six people for a week—six people who had spent most of their time on the beach, judging by the amount of sand Phyllida swept up. They had also spent a lot of time eating and drinking. She had to rescrub most of the pots, and the barbecue that had been fixed to the back of the boat was so disgusting that she put it aside to clean properly when she had hot water and a decent pair of rubber gloves.

She gathered up dirty bedlinen, wiped down sinks and shelves, contorted herself into impossible positions to clean out every nook and cranny she could find, scrubbed the stove until it gleamed and swept every inch of the floor. When it go so hot that she couldn't bear it any more, she climbed up the companionway to dump a pile of bedding in the cockpit and feel the blessedly cool breeze against her skin for a moment.

Her face was bright red, her hair sticking unpleasantly to the back of her neck. She felt as limp as a wrung rag, and the sight of Jake looking relaxed on the neighbouring boat did nothing to improve her temper. He was sitting on the raised edge of the cockpit, his feet on the lockers, polishing some metal parts with a grubby rag. The sun was dancing on the water around him, the boat rocking gently in the breeze. He looked cool and comfortable and completely at home.

'I see you believe in setting an example of hard work to your staff,' she said acidly, dropping the bedding onto the lockers.

Jake eyed her dishevelled appearance with some amusement. She was hardly recognisable as the girl in the smart suit who had stood at the check-in desk at Adelaide airport. Instead she looked hot and tired and decidedly cross.

'I need to be able to hear the radio and the phone,' he explained, laying down his rag. 'I could sit in the office, but I might as well be out here doing something useful.'

'You could hear them down there,' said Phyllida, pointing down into the hot cabin. 'And then *I* could have a nice time sitting on deck in the sun!'

'Do you know how to put a winch back together again?' said Jake in a deceptively pleasant tone, gesturing at the bits of metal around his feet.

'No.'

'That's why you're down there and I'm up here.' Picking up his rag, he calmly resumed his polishing. 'If you want a cushier job, Phyllida, you're going to have to learn a bit more about boats.'

'I'm learning quite enough about boats down here, thank you,' she grumbled, disappearing back down the companionway.

At last she had finished. Struggling wearily up the steps with her bucket, Phyllida tipped the dirty water over the side, and stashed all her materials back inside before sarcastically inviting Jake over for an inspection.

He came, moving with the ease and unselfconscious grace of a cat between the two boats. Phyllida thought of her own clumsy boarding and hated him. She watched, simmering, as Jake methodically checked the cabins.

'You haven't cleaned the fridge—it's still full of water. And the lockers beneath the seats are a mess, but otherwise . . . not bad.'

Not bad! Phyllida blew her damp fringe off her forehead and glowered at him. She had never worked so hard before in her life, and all he could say was 'not bad'!

'That's just below deck,' he added, climbing up to where she sat limply in the cockpit. 'There's still the decks and the cockpit up here to be scrubbed, and the inventory will have to be checked as well.'

Phyllida stared at him, aghast. 'What, now?' She didn't feel as if she could stand up, let alone contemplate another cleaning marathon.

Jake frowned. 'Tomorrow. You look as if you've been hit by a ten-ton truck. Are you all right?'

'I do feel a bit odd, now you mention it,' said Phyllida. She had felt fine until she'd sat down, but a wave of exhaustion had suddenly engulfed her, leaving her feeling quite light-headed.

'Jet lag,' said Jake tersely. 'That's all we need!'

'I'll be perfectly all right if I just sit down for five minutes,' she said, determined not to give him any excuse for accusing her of being weak and pathetic, but Jake simply ignored her and lifted her bodily to her feet.

'Come on, I'd better get you home.'

'To Chris's house,' she reminded him. She wouldn't put it past Jake to take advantage of her state to get his own way.

Jake sighed. 'Oh, all right. To Chris's house, if you must.' He glanced at her. 'Are you always this stubborn?'

'I'm not some slave you've just acquired,' she told him. 'I've got a mind of my own.'

'Pity you don't use it, then,' said Jake acidly. 'I'll take you back to Chris's now, but this is the last time. You'll have to get yourself in to the marina tomorrow—and if you expect me to subsidise you for taxis, you've got another think coming.'

'I won't need a taxi,' Phyllida told him loftily as he pulled up outside Chris's house. She couldn't wait to get to bed, but after she'd got out and closed the door behind her she leant back through the open window. The brown eyes were clouded with tiredness, but there was no mistaking the challenge in their gaze. 'I'm going to walk.'

CHAPTER FIVE

'YOU'RE late!'

Phyllida collapsed against the door of the office and eyed Jake with acute hostility. It hadn't taken her long that morning to regret her proud boast about walking in. Deep sleep had left her feeling woozy and sluggish, and she had been reaching for the phone to call a taxi when she had remembered that in her rush to get from Adelaide to Port Lincoln she hadn't had time to change any money.

Chris had given her what she could, but it had only just been enough for yesterday's taxi to the marina as it was. It looked as if she was going to have to walk after all.

Now she pushed her fringe wearily out of her eyes and wondered if she looked as hot and bothered as she felt. 'I'm sorry, but it's taken me over an hour to get here,' she told Jake.

It had seemed twice as long as she toiled along the wide, empty streets, wincing as her shoes rubbed against feet that were still tender from the other night. At least she had remembered to wear a hat. She fanned herself with it in an effort to cool her pink face.

Jake was predictably unsympathetic. 'You should have taken that into account before you insisted on walking,' he said. 'You'll just have to leave an hour earlier tomorrow morning. I've got people coming in to charter three of those boats the day after tomorrow, and they won't be ready if you swan in at this time every day.'

'I've said I'm sorry,' said Phyllida through gritted teeth, pulling off her shoes to rub her sore feet. 'I won't be late tomorrow.'

'You'd better not be,' said Jake in a steel-edged voice. 'If you want to keep this job for Chris, you're going to have to do better than you've done so far. Now, you can start by finishing off *Calypso*, and then move on to *Valli* and *Dora Dee*.'

Phyllida's face was bright with anger as she snatched up the cleaning bucket and stalked down the jetty. She longed to tell Jake what he could do with his job, but Chris had rung last night, and had sounded so tired and anxious about Mike that not for the world would Phyllida add to her worries.

She was just going to have to learn to put up with Jake—although she had been furious to learn that Chris had already spoken to him and had been enthusiastic about the idea of Phyllida moving into his house.

'I'd feel so much better to know that you were with Jake instead of stuck out there on your own,' she had said. 'It's a lovely house, and he's promised to look after you for me.'

Oh, he had, had he? Phyllida had told Chris that she would see, but she had vowed to show Jake once and for all that she didn't need to be looked after—least of all by him!

Now, fury carried her over the guard rails without her stopping to think about falling into the water. She found scrubbing the decks a useful therapy too, and finished cleaning *Calypso* in double-quick time before refilling her water bucket and clambering across onto *Valli*. It wasn't the most elegant of manoeuvres, but at least she did it by herself.

Phyllida scoured and swept and polished with a sort of concentrated fury, imagining Jake's face beneath her scrubbing brush and wishing she could as easily scrub away the memory of that wretched kiss. The feel of his lips, the touch of his hands, the dark throb of excitement...

The memories lurked annoyingly, ready to drift across Phyllida's mind when she least suspected it, and making her falter in what she was doing. That only made her crosser than ever, and she would scrub even harder, but the time passed more quickly than she would have believed possible.

She could hardly believe it when Jake hailed her from the jetty and she sat back on her heels to see that it was one o'clock. 'Come and have some lunch,' he said. 'It's time you had a break.'

Phyllida wiped her forehead with the back of her arm. She had successfully scrubbed out her anger, and could see now that she had been really rather silly in blaming everything on Jake. After all, she was the one who had been over an hour late.

'I haven't got any money,' she said, getting to her feet a little stiffly. 'Is there a bank nearby where I can change some?'

'You can do that when we go and buy the provisions tomorrow,' said Jake. 'I'll buy you lunch today. You look as if you could do with a good square meal. When was the last time you ate?'

'I had some fruit for breakfast, but I wasn't very hungry last night.' Phyllida was almost getting used to climbing on and off boats by now, and she stepped down beside Jake without mishap. 'I suppose I haven't had a proper meal since the plane.'

'You can hardly call airline food a proper meal,' Jake grunted. 'We'll go up to the marina restaurant.'

'I can't go to a restaurant dressed like this!' Phyllida protested, gesturing down at the shorts and T-shirt she

had put on because they were the only things she didn't
mind getting dirty. Just as well, too, as they were already
splashed and stained and more than a little grimy.

'This isn't exactly a five-star restaurant,' said Jake
sardonically. 'There's no need to panic. You look fine.'
He paused, watching Phyllida tie the laces of her canvas
shoes.

In spite of the damp patches, the yellow T-shirt and
white shorts looked fresh and summery, somehow em-
phasising her gamine quality. She hadn't bothered to
blowdry her hair into its usual sleek bob, and instead it
fell in a shiny, rather tangled mop around her face.

'In fact,' he went on slowly as she straightened, 'you
look very nice—much better than you did in that ridiculous suit. That smart, sophisticated image obviously
wasn't the real you.'

'Yes, it was!' She ruffled up instantly, obscurely piqued
by that tepid 'very nice'. Hardly the most effusive of
compliments! 'You may not think much of dressing
smartly, but in my job what you look like is important.'

'Then perhaps your job isn't the real you either?'

'It is,' she insisted. Working at Pritchard Price had
been all-absorbing. It had been stimulating, challenging, fun... everything a job should have been, and
she had loved it. 'It's the most important thing about
me.'

Jake looked at her. 'I'd have said that the most important thing about you was the fact that you're prepared to get down on your hands and knees and tackle
a hard, dirty job to help your cousin out,' he said, and
headed up the steps leading up from the jetty.

Puzzled, Phyllida stared after him. She found Jake
very confusing. It was typical of him to disagree with
her so absolutely, but surely that had been a genuine
note of respect in his voice?

Rupert had always had a smooth line in compliments, she remembered. In fact, once or twice she had suspected that he flattered her automatically, without actually seeing what she was wearing or tasting what she had cooked. It would be much harder to win a compliment from a man like Jake. Perhaps she hadn't done so badly with 'very nice' after all!

As Jake had promised, the restaurant was far from formal, but the food was delicious. They sat outside, on a terrace overlooking the marina, and Phyllida thought she had rarely enjoyed a meal more. When a platter of local seafood arrived with a crisp salad, she suddenly discovered that she was ravenous.

Jake watched her apply herself to her food with amusement. 'Do you do everything with such fierce determination?' He grinned.

Guiltily, Phyllida realised that she had been bolting her food in a most undignified way. 'I didn't realise I was so hungry,' she apologised.

'Oh, it's not just the way you eat. I've noticed it in the way you set about cleaning as well. You were a small fury on the boats this morning—I thought you were going to scrub through the fibreglass!'

'That was because—' Phyllida stopped. She could hardly tell Jake that she had spent the entire morning thinking about him. 'I've always been a believer in the "do a job, do it properly" philosophy,' she improvised. It was true, anyway. She had always hated not being good at things, and would far rather not do anything at all than be bad at it.

'It's all or nothing for you, isn't it, Phyllida?'

'I suppose you could say that,' she said, returning her attention to her plate. 'I'm certainly prepared to give everything to whatever job I'm doing.'

'And what about love? Do you throw yourself as wholeheartedly into that, or are you too busy pursuing your precious career?'

Jake's voice held the same bitter edge she had heard in it once or twice before, and she glanced at him curiously. His knuckles were tight around his glass, and the green eyes had darkened to grey, but the contemptuous expression vanished when he saw that she was watching him.

'What's it to you?' she asked suspiciously.

'Just wondering whether you conform to type, that's all.'

'What type?'

'A type of obsessive career woman, determined to succeed whatever it costs.'

'That's absolute rubbish!' said Phyllida scornfully. 'What do you know about career women, anyway?'

'Quite a lot. I was married to one for five years.'

Married? Phyllida put down her knife and fork, shaken by the depth of her own reaction at the idea of Jake living with another woman, loving her, laughing with her. 'I didn't know you'd been married,' she said unsteadily.

'It wasn't an experience I'm anxious to repeat,' said Jake. 'My wife was far more in love with her career than she was with me.'

Phyllida remembered her own discovery that losing her job meant more to her than losing Rupert, and she shifted a little uneasily in her chair. 'Perhaps she wanted a fulfilling career as well as you?' she said, justifying her own position as much as Jake's unknown wife's— although it was hard to imagine feeling like that about Jake.

His wife must have been very dedicated to have put her career before him. Or was that just Jake being a typical man and resenting a woman's success? 'Men are allowed to have a career and a marriage. Why can't it be the same for women? It ought to be possible to have both.'

'Of course,' he said. 'But that only works as long as the career doesn't develop into an obsession that denies a place to the other things that matter in life.'

'That's good, coming from a man who prefers boats to women!'

Jake laughed suddenly. 'Don't worry, Phyllida. I allow myself plenty of time to devote to other interests—including women!'

'What you do in your spare time is hardly likely to be a source of concern to me,' said Phyllida frigidly and not entirely truthfully.

'Of course not,' said Jake, but his eyes seemed to dance with a laughter that tugged at Phyllida's heart.

Dropping her gaze, she concentrated fiercely on her plate, but the look in his eyes continued to shimmer in her mind. She felt edgy, confused. One minute she could swear that he despised her, the next she was sure that he was coming to like her in spite of herself. The fact that she felt exactly the same about him was somehow not reassuring.

She didn't despise him, exactly, but she had always loathed chauvinistic men who were full of good reasons for women not pursuing a career just as vigorously as men. The fact that Rupert had so unexpectedly turned out to be one of them only made things worse. And Jake had none of Rupert's other advantages to compensate; he wasted no time on charm or flattery, he was disagreeable and deliberately provocative at times, he made no secret of the fact that he found her alternately exasperating and faintly ridiculous...

And yet...

There *was* something intriguing about him, Phyllida admitted to herself reluctantly. He made no effort to impress. She was even beginning to wonder if she had imagined the wealthy executive she had first met at Adelaide airport, with his briefcase and subtly expensive clothes. Now he seemed quite at home in jeans and a casual shirt, and seemed happy to spend his day greasing winches or taking an engine to bits.

It didn't fit at all with Phyllida's idea of how a man who owned a fleet of yachts—not to mention a plane and an enormous four-wheel drive—ought to behave. From what Chris had told her money wasn't a problem, and he must have a shrewd sense of business if he ran his own company as well as the vast Tregowan interests in South Australia.

Why didn't he pay someone else to mend the engine, or do the paperwork? And if he wouldn't have a secretary, why didn't he at least buy himself a mobile phone so that he didn't have to run down the jetty whenever the phone rang in the office? Not that Phyllida had ever seen him run. If the phone did ring, he would wipe his hands on a rag, step off the boat and walk in that infuriatingly unhurried way of his down to the office.

Phyllida had watched him on at least three occasions that morning, and had longed for the phone to stop ringing just as he reached it, but of course it never did. If it had been her, she would have leapt off the boat and belted to the phone only to find the caller had hung up when she got there, but they went on ringing patiently for Jake. It was very unfair.

Phyllida was stiff and weary by the time she had finished cleaning that afternoon. She found Jake sitting in the office for once, checking through some booking forms, but when she asked if there was anything else he wanted her to do he shook his head and told her that she'd done enough for the day.

'You go on home,' he said absently, half his mind still on the forms.

Phyllida hesitated. If she could have been transported by magic carpet back to Chris's home, she would have been delighted to take him up on his offer. As it was, she still didn't have any money, and as Jake obviously wasn't going to offer her a lift it looked as if she would have to embark on the long trek back on her sore feet. It was not an inviting prospect.

Still, she had better get on with it, or she would never get back at all. Silently cursing the stubbornness that had made her insist on staying at Chris's house, Phyllida wished Jake a frosty goodbye, squared her shoulders and set off across the marina.

The morning's breeze had died out, and it was hot and still. She limped out to the main road and stood looking down to where it curved off in a faint haze of heat. There seemed to be very little traffic around, only a van, which sped past her in the opposite direction with a brief blast of its horn—although whether it was in warning or tribute, Phyllida couldn't tell.

She looked helplessly up and down the road. From what she had seen so far, the streets seemed to be permanently empty. Didn't the Australians ever go out in their cars? Or were there just not enough of them to fill up the available space? Whatever, it didn't look as if she was even going to get a lift into town.

Phyllida sighed, and began to walk down the road. Then she stopped abruptly. 'This is ridiculous!' she said out loud, and, turning on her heel, she trudged back into the marina, along the jetty, back to the little wooden office and Jake.

He was leaning back in his chair, long legs propped up on the desk, but he put down the list he was studying as Phyllida slunk in the door. 'Forgotten something?'

'No.' Having got this far, she couldn't quite think what she was going to say next.

'In that case, what can I do for you?' Jake knew why she was here, Phyllida was certain. His face might be deadpan, not even the slightest curl to his mouth, but the grey-green eyes were alight with the ironically amused expression that always made her prickle with an unsettling mixture of confusion and hostility and deep, shameful longing to see him smile properly—at her. At her alone.

As usual, Phyllida let the hostility win. It was easier that way. 'You can stop being hateful and disagreeable for a start!' she snapped, dropping into a chair. 'You must know perfectly well why I've come back. And before you start, I'll say it all for you!'

She looked him straight in the eye, holding up her hand as he opened his mouth to speak, and all at once her anger faded.

'I've already refused your offer to have me to stay in no uncertain terms, and I have absolutely no right to ask you to invite me again. I've been stubborn and unreasonable and rude ever since we first met, and I quite agree that it's entirely my own fault if I'm so tired now that I can't walk another step.

'But if we could take all that as read, will you believe me if I say that I really am very sorry I've been so stupid and ungracious, and could I please take you up on your very generous offer to let me stay with you after all?'

Jake swung his legs down to the floor, the mocking look in his eyes replaced by one much harder to read. 'Your feet *must* be hurting!' he teased, but there was a warmer note in his voice, and instead of ruffling up as she usually did, Phyllida found herself remembering suddenly what had happened the last time her feet had hurt.

'They are,' she said unsteadily.

'I suspect I owe you an apology too,' said Jake unexpectedly. 'Being handed a bucket of cleaning materials and being told to get on with it probably wasn't the welcome to Australia you imagined.'

'Nothing's been as I imagined,' Phyllida admitted a little ruefully. 'If it had been, maybe I wouldn't have been behaving so out of character. I'm not usually this touchy.' She hesitated. 'I'm not proud of the way I behaved the other night either. I never cry and carry on like that. Do you think you could forget it and pretend that we've just met?'

'I'm not sure that I can forget *quite* everything,' said Jake slowly, his eyes resting on her mouth. He made no move to touch her, but suddenly it was as if the memory of that kiss was a tangible thing again, strumming in the air between them. 'Can you?'

Phyllida could feel a trembling start deep inside her, and she was very glad that she was sitting down. This is ridiculous, she told herself desperately. He's only looking at you; he isn't even touching you. There's absolutely no reason for your bones to melt and your skin to tingle and your heart to start booming in your ears. It was just a silly kiss to snap you out of hysterics. It didn't mean anything.

She really must get a hold of herself.

'I'm prepared to try if you are,' she said, appalled at how husky her voice sounded. She cleared her throat awkwardly. Honestly, anyone would think she'd never been kissed before!

'Let's agree on a fresh start, then,' said Jake, leaning forward and holding out his hand. 'Shall we shake on it?'

He was doing this deliberately! Didn't he know how much the touch of his fingers disturbed her? Couldn't he feel her shiver of response? Phyllida steeled herself and took his hand, but when she would have withdrawn it he tightened his hold and drew her to her feet. For one crazy, exhilarating, terrifying moment she thought he was going to kiss her, but he only looked down at their linked hands.

'You're right about one thing, though, Phyllida.'

'What's that?' she croaked.

'You're a lot tougher than you look. It takes guts to admit that you've been wrong, as you did just now, but if it's any consolation, I'm beginning to think I might have been wrong about you too.'

Phyllida sat on the veranda and twisted the wine glass around in her hand as she gazed unseeingly down at the lights of the marina, shimmering reflections over the dark water.

She was glad she had apologised to Jake, but, instead of clearing the air, it had served only to tighten the atmosphere between them during the course of the evening.

Phyllida was excruciatingly aware of Jake, of his fingers around the wine bottle, of the easy, unhurried way he lifted his arm or turned his head, of the whole warm, solid strength of him. She tried not to look at him—whenever she did she felt as if the air was being squeezed slowly but surely out of her lungs. And if it carried on this way, she soon wouldn't be able to breathe at all.

It wasn't supposed to be like this. She had thought that starting afresh would give her the opportunity to prove to Jake just how poised and professional she really was. Instead, she had ended up as tongue-tied and awkward as a schoolgirl on her first date.

Jake had driven her out to Chris's to pick up her case, and then back to this lovely airy house set on the hill, looking down to the marina on one side and out to Boston Island and the distant sea on the other. Phyllida had liked it as soon as she'd walked into its cool, uncluttered rooms, with their polished wooden floors and the long windows opening out onto the wide, shaded veranda.

Jake was as competent in the kitchen as anywhere else. He'd thrown together a salad and barbecued some fish outside on the veranda, reminding Phyllida that he was a man used to looking after himself. She'd watched his face, lit from beneath by a lantern which stood on the wall by the barbecue, and tried to imagine him in a life of happy domesticity.

He must have been happy at some time with his wife, but there was such a detached, independent quality in him now that it was impossible to picture him giving up his freedom again for the dubious prospect of matrimony. Unthinkingly, Phyllida had sighed.

Now she searched her mind for something to say. Jake seemed quite unbothered by the long, sticky silences, but for Phyllida they were agony. The marina lights danced in front of her eyes, but she couldn't mention them again. She had already commented on the view, on the temperature, on the wine, and was convinced that he must think her irredeemably boring and superficial.

The phone ringing in the room behind her was an enormous relief. Jake got up to answer it, and she could tell from what he was saying that he was talking to Chris. Well, that at least would be something else to talk about.

'Yes, I'll tell her,' she heard him say just before he put the phone down. 'That was Chris,' he confirmed as he came back out onto the veranda. No surprise, no sudden movement, but still Phyllida felt the same tightening of breath at his reappearance. 'I told her you had moved in and she sounded very relieved. She sends her love.'

'How's Mike?'

'Still in Intensive Care, but he's recovered consciousness, so that's a good sign. Chris is sounding a lot more cheerful.'

'Does she have any idea how long he'll have to stay in hospital?'

Jake sat down beside her and looked thoughtfully across at the marina. 'Not yet.' He glanced at her. 'I'm afraid you may have to resign yourself to quite a long stay here.'

'Oh, dear.'

'It's not much of a holiday for you, is it?'

'It's not that,' said Phyllida hesitantly, acutely conscious of him sitting so close beside her.

Her hand was resting on the arm of the wicker chair. She would only have to lift her hand, move it three inches and she could touch his. Her fingers were tingling at the thought, and she pulled her hands down into her lap and linked them together, as if afraid that they might start drifting towards him of their own accord.

'I was thinking about you. You probably didn't bank on having me to stay for such a long time when you offered.'

Jake turned to look at her, his mouth just curling into something that was almost, but not quite a smile. 'No, I must admit that I didn't bank on you...'

There was an odd pause, and Phyllida felt her eyes dragged unwillingly to meet his. She didn't want to look at him, didn't want the trembling inside to build into an insistent, booming rhythm, didn't want him to see that beneath her proud boasts of toughness and independence she was just as vulnerable as anyone else. She couldn't breathe, couldn't move, could only stare back at him, helplessly entangled in a tightening web of awareness.

'There's no problem, though,' Jake continued softly. 'As you can see, there's plenty of room here, so you're welcome to make yourself at home for as long as you want.'

'Thank you,' said Phyllida with a sort of gasp, expelling the last air from her lungs.

With a superhuman effort she lunged to her feet, seriously alarmed by her own bizarre behaviour and desperate in case she succumbed to the terrible temptation of reaching out and touching him. She didn't understand what was happening to her, but she knew that if she didn't get away right now she would do something she would regret.

To her horror, Jake rose to his feet with her. 'Where are you going?'

'I...I thought I'd—er—go and write some letters home,' stammered Phyllida.

'To your fiancé?' His voice was suddenly hard.

Surprise stopped Phyllida in her tracks. 'My fiancé?'

'Chris talks about you a lot. I've heard all about her famous English cousin. How important your job is, how smartly your flat is decorated...how you've got yourself engaged to some smooth charmer who's got everything going for him.'

If she hadn't known better, Phyllida would have suspected that the sneering, almost hostile tone was a cover for jealousy.

'You've had plenty to say about your job, but you've kept very quiet about your engagement. Why's that, Phyllida?'

'The subject hasn't come up,' she said uneasily. She could have told Jake that she had no intention of marrying Rupert, but some instinct told her that she would be much safer pretending that the engagement was still on.

'We were talking about love only this lunchtime—or don't you associate love with your fiancé?'

'Of course I do,' she said coldly, grateful to him for the hostility that had sprung back into the atmosphere. It was much, much easier to argue with him than to notice the way the light caught his cheek and the line of his jaw. 'Rupert's very special to me, and I didn't feel like discussing him with *you*, that's all.'

'*Rupert*?' Jake jeered, mimicking her English accent. 'Is that really his name?'

'What's wrong with Rupert?' she demanded in a frigid voice.

'It's very...English.'

'I realise that that may place him at a terrible disadvantage in your eyes, but it doesn't in mine. It may have escaped your notice, but I am English too.'

'I could hardly avoid noticing,' said Jake. 'Even before you open your mouth it's obvious—in the way you lift that stubborn little chin of yours and look down your nose!'

'In that case you'll probably agree that Rupert and I suit each other perfectly!'

'I don't know about that. I'd have said you needed a man with a stronger will than yours—and there can't be many of those about!'

Only a minute ago, Phyllida had been desperate with nerves; now she was blazing with temper. 'What makes you think you know what Rupert's like?'

'Well, if you were my fiancé, I wouldn't let you go gallivanting off to Australia without me. I'd want you right where I could keep an eye on you!'

'Perhaps Rupert trusts me?' Phyllida suggested sweetly. 'Perhaps he admires and encourages my independence—which is more than you obviously did for your wife!'

It was an unfair shot, and Jake's eyes narrowed, but he didn't rise to the bait. 'So Rupert trusts you, does he? Would he still trust you, I wonder, if he knew you were staying here alone with me?'

Phyllida strongly suspected that if they had still been engaged, Rupert would have been intensely suspicious of the whole set-up, but she had no intention of telling Jake *that*. 'Naturally,' she said. 'I'm just about to write and tell him where I am, and what you're like, and that ought to be quite enough to reassure him that he has absolutely no cause for concern!'

She should have known better, of course. If she hadn't been so alarmed by the reactions which had left her stammering and stuttering like a schoolgirl, she wouldn't have been nearly so angry. And if she hadn't been angry she wouldn't have let slip a comment that was bound to goad Jake, who for some reason was nearly as angry as she was.

'It sounds like a very dull letter,' he sneered, moving purposefully towards her.

Phyllida tried to sidestep round the table, but the chair got in her way and she ended up pinned against the veranda rail, her eyes huge and dark and defiant.

'We don't want Rupert to think you're not having a good time in Australia.' He took her face in his hands, feathering his thumbs along the line of her cheekbones and studying her features almost impersonally, like a connoisseur. Quite suddenly, he smiled. 'I think we should find something more exciting for you to write home about, don't you?'

Phyllida never had the chance to reply. His hands tightened and then his mouth was on hers and he was kissing her, long and hard, with a sort of suppressed fury that dissolved almost instantly into intense, unmistakable and utterly unexpected passion. It shook them both off balance.

Jake lifted his head and looked down into Phyllida's face as if he had never seen her before. She stared dazedly back up at him, as confused as he was about the explosion of feeling that had thrilled through her at the first touch of his lips. Her body was glowing, afire with new and dangerous sensations, and her mind was spinning, half frightened by the depth of her reaction, half frantic because Jake had stopped just as she had yielded.

For a long, long moment, they just stared at each other, then Jake's hold slackened. Certain that he was going to step away, Phyllida was conscious of an alarming stab of disappointment before he seemed to change his mind, letting his hands fall from her face only to jerk her abruptly back into his arms.

With a tiny sigh of release, she melted against him, all anger and frustration forgotten. Her lips were soft and sweet beneath his, savouring the same poignant rush of intoxicating pleasure, sharing the same breathless urgency as his arms tightened around her.

She had been clutching him just above the elbow—at first with some vague notion of pulling his hands down from her face, then as her one solid anchor in the tur-

bulent whirl of emotions. Now she let them slide luxuriously down his sides.

His body was so hard, so strong. She could feel the
taut muscles flexing through the thin cotton of his shirt
as she ran her hands over him, down to his waist and
around him to spread over his back, pulling him closer,
desperate to feel the solidity and the strength and the
sheer power of him.

Heedless of the veranda rail digging into the small of
her back, Phyllida murmured deep in her throat with
delight and a half conscious disbelief at her own lack of
control. Somewhere at the back of her mind a voice was
urging her to pull away, before it was too late, but she
was lost, tumbling and turning helplessly in a swirling
tide of sensation as Jake's lips plundered hers, and Jake's
hands slid in insistent exploration over her slenderness,
and Jake's body pressed hard and demanding against
her.

His mouth was drifting down her throat, his fingers
brushing aside the soft material of her skirt to spread
over the smooth length of her thigh, his warm hand
sliding possessively upwards, until Phyllida gasped at the
excruciating twist of desire.

Very slowly, Jake lifted his head, letting his lips travel
in final salute along the proud, pure jawline before his
hand dropped reluctantly and he smoothed her skirt back
into place. In the dim light his eyes gleamed as he put
her carefully away from him.

'Give my regards to Rupert when you write,' he said,
a little unevenly. 'He's either a very brave man or a
very stupid one to let a girl like you out on her own!'
And, turning, he walked away into the house without
another word.

CHAPTER SIX

THE kiss was never referred to by either of them over the next three weeks. Shaken, bewildered, appalled by her own behaviour, Phyllida lay awake long into the night. How could she have let him kiss her like that? How could she have kissed him back?

She burned with humiliation as the kiss replayed itself over and over again in her mind. She could still feel the sharp thrill of excitement when Jake had pulled her into his arms, the warm persuasion of his lips and the searing pleasure of his hand smoothing up her thigh.

If it had just been that, she could have channelled her shock into anger against Jake. It would have been easy to have blamed him... But it was impossible to forget how she had revelled in the feel of his body beneath her hands, how she had explored his lips with her own and gasped with delight at his touch. Jake wasn't responsible for that, was he?

Phyllida had many faults, but self-deception wasn't one of them. She was just as much to blame as Jake, and she knew it. The fact made her angrier than ever, but much as she would have liked a blazing argument with him, a night's reflection told her that it would be much more dignified to ignore the whole incident. She would be cool and quellingly polite, and with any luck Jake would begin to wonder whether he had imagined the warm, passionate girl he had held in his arms.

It was unfortunate that the weeks that followed were extremely busy ones. Phyllida wrote out long lists of ingredients, sorted out piles of provisions for each boat, and spent long hours simmering fragrant stews in Jake's kitchen. Jake rarely disturbed her there, and it was easy to tell herself that she had succeeded in putting the kiss firmly behind her.

It was a little more difficult when she was down at the marina. There were boats to be cleaned, brochures to be posted, queries to be answered and stores to be sorted, but, no matter how much she had to do, she never quite managed to ignore Jake the way she wanted to be able to.

He was always around, always as busy as she was, but somehow managing to move with the same deliberate, unhurried competence. Phyllida couldn't help feeling brittle and frazzled in comparison.

She didn't know whether to feel relieved or outraged the morning after the kiss, when Jake behaved as if precisely nothing had happened. He continued to treat her with a blend of amusement and faint exasperation, and if his heart stuck in his throat every time she walked into the room—as hers did whenever he appeared—he gave not the slightest sign of it.

Phyllida bitterly resented the effortless way he seemed able to carry on exactly as before. She was finding it much harder. True, she was quite proud of her cool manner, but Jake didn't appear in the slightest bit quelled, and she doubted whether he even noticed. Frustrated by her own inability to impress on him how completely she had forgotten the kiss, Phyllida threw herself into the task of preparing the boats.

As the days passed, and it became obvious that Jake wasn't going to allude to the kiss any more than she was, her embarrassment faded, and with it her frosty manner. Sometimes she forgot about the kiss altogether, and would talk and laugh with him quite easily until her unwary eyes would fall upon his hands or his mouth, and memory would come rushing back.

She grew to love the casual life down at the marina—the jostling boats and the sound of the wind in the rigging and the clear, sharp light. She liked the easy camaraderie of the yachtsmen who stopped to talk to Jake, and envied the confident way they jumped into their boats and pulled up flapping sails as they headed out to sea.

Phyllida found them friendly and fun, and felt increasingly conscious of the fact that she didn't belong. She couldn't talk about luffing or gybing or flogging sails, and stories about mizzens, genoas, spinnakers and storm jibs were frankly baffling. She was constantly getting into trouble from Jake for talking about the beds instead of the bunks, ropes instead of sheets, cupboards instead of lockers, and when she overheard him telling someone that she wouldn't know a reef-knot from a rudder, she decided it was high time she improved her knowledge.

The next time Jake took her into town to stock up on provisions, she slipped off and bought herself a book on sailing for beginners, determined to show Jake that she wasn't as stupid as he thought her. She took to studying it in secret, but it didn't make a lot of sense without a boat to practise on. She spent her day surrounded by yachts, but was much too busy ever to learn more than just how dirty a boat could get in a week.

'Ah, Phyllida, just the girl I want!' said Jake one day as she walked into the office, her arms full of dirty linen. He held up the radio microphone. 'I've got *Valli* on the radio. They've discovered a Tupperware box full of bits of dill and want to know what it's for.'

Phyllida put her bundle down on a chair. 'It's for garnish,' she said, surprised at the question.

'Garnish?' said Jake, dropping his head into his hand. 'Now, why didn't I think of that?'

His sarcasm went over Phyllida's head. 'Well, I must say, I'd have thought it was obvious.'

'Not to four men who are out for a couple of days' fishing,' said Jake sardonically. 'I thought I told you just to make sure they had plenty of beer, some bread and a few potatoes?'

'I did all that, but as you said they'd just be eating fish I thought it would be nice if they had some dill with it—you know, a bit of greenery.'

'Phyllida, this lot aren't interested in the artistic combinations on their plate! You're not catering for a five-star restaurant. If you're out on a sailing trip, you want good, nourishing food and lots of it, not to be poncing around with garnishes! Have you been giving these extras to everyone?'

'Yes,' said Phyllida defensively. 'Dill's very nice with fish. They don't have to use it as a garnish, if that's too subtle for them. They can stuff the fish with it, or chop it up and mix it with mayonnaise...'

'Spare me the recipes,' said Jake holding up a hand. 'I don't think I want to know!' He turned back to the radio. '*Valli*, this is Sailaway. I'm reliably informed that you are indeed supposed to have the box of dill. Phyllida tells me that you can mix it with mayonnaise, or alternatively use it as a garnish. Over.'

There was a baffled silence, and then a voice crackled back, evidently much amused. 'We'll give it a go. And if your Phyllida made the stew we had last night, tell her it was fantastic! We wished we'd asked for one for both nights. This is *Valli*, over and out.'

'Sailaway out, and standing by.' Jake put the microphone down and shook his head at Phyllida. 'Garnishes! What next? Cocktails and canapés?'

Phyllida brightened. 'That's a good idea. We could—'

'No, we couldn't,' Jake interrupted her with a flat note of finality, but his eyes held a lurking smile. 'My reputation might just be able to stand rumours of garnish, but I draw the line at canapés. Do you want to make me a laughing stock of the yachting world?'

She sighed. 'I don't seem to be able to get anything right, do I?'

'That doesn't sound like you, Phyllida.' Pushing back his chair, Jake got to his feet. 'What happened to all that confident defiance? You swore you'd prove you were tougher than you looked, and you have.' He paused, the smile fading from his expression as he looked down into her wary face.

'You've worked really hard over the last three weeks, Phyllida. You heard what *Valli* said just now, and it's not the first time I've been told how good the food is. I didn't think you'd stick at it,' he went on slowly, 'but I was wrong.'

His eyes were very green. Phyllida stood quite still, but a quiver was spreading out from her heart, shivering down to her fingertips and toes, until her whole body vibrated with it.

The atmosphere was taut with a new and unspoken tension. Jake took a deliberate step towards her, and the silence tightened, only to snap abruptly as a huge, bearded figure appeared in the doorway.

'Jake, you didn't tell me you'd got a new assistant!'

'Rod.' Jake seemed to recover himself with an effort, and shook the stranger's hand. 'I wasn't expecting you so soon.'

'I got an earlier flight,' said the man, regarding Phyllida with undisguised interest. 'I didn't think you'd mind me turning up early, and now I'm glad I did. Aren't you going to introduce us?'

It seemed to Phyllida that Jake performed the introductions with some reserve. 'Phyllida, this is Rod Franklin. He's going to skipper *Persephone* for the party arriving tomorrow. Rod, Phyllida Grant.' He told Rod about Mike's accident and how Phyllida was standing in for Chris.

'That's bad luck on Mike,' said Rod, enveloping Phyllida's hand in a massive paw. He had a jovial face and merry blue eyes. 'But good luck for the rest of us! Have you done much sailing before?'

'Phyllida's still learning the difference between the bow and the stern,' said Jake unfairly, glowering at Phyllida, who found herself snatching her hand out of Rod's.

Cross with herself for reacting so quickly to his look, Phyllida turned a brilliant smile on Rod. 'I'd like to learn, though.'

'Of course you would,' said Rod, delighted. 'My party don't arrive until tomorrow afternoon. I could take you out tomorrow morning if you like?'

Phyllida opened her mouth to reply, but Jake, who was suddenly looking boot-faced, got in first. 'She's got too much to do tomorrow,' he said flatly.

'Oh, well . . .' Rod looked from one to the other in puzzlement. 'Another time, then?'

'I'll look forward to it,' said Phyllida sweetly, before Jake could answer for her again.

'You've never told me that you wanted to learn to sail,' he accused her when Rod had disappeared up to the house with his bags.

'You've never asked me,' she retorted, picking up the linen from the chair and dumping it in the laundry bag. The warmth that had shimmered between them before Rod's appearance had vanished, submerged by the more

familiar antagonism. Jake might have admitted that he
had been wrong about her, but it obviously didn't stop
him treating her like some slave! 'You don't need to
worry,' she reassured him acidly. 'I haven't forgotten that
I'm here to work, not to enjoy myself!'

It had been arranged that Rod was to spend the night
at Jake's house, and he was patently delighted to discover that Phyllida was staying there as well. She found
him good company, with an endless fund of stories, and
although many of them were about sailing, even she
could appreciate most of them. It should have been an
entertaining evening, but Jake was out of humour.

He did insist on taking them both out to dinner, de-
creeing that Phyllida had done enough cooking, but her
enjoyment was soured when she discovered that he had
invited a friend of his to join them for dinner.

It curdled completely when she met the friend, a tall,
statuesque blonde called Val, who might have been
chosen expressly to provide a contrast to Phyllida. Val
had a fresh prettiness and a totally natural look that was
like Chris's, but which somehow lacked her cousin's
warmth and humour.

Val, Phyllida soon discovered, was an expert sailor,
and had been one of an all-female crew on the Sydney-
Hobart that had just taken place. It didn't take long to
realise that the other girl also had a distinct interest in
Jake, although whether he was aware of it or not wasn't
nearly as obvious.

It wouldn't be surprising, Phyllida decided glumly. Val
was far more his type than a dark, slender career girl
who didn't know the first thing about sailing. She found
the thought oddly depressing.

Edged deliberately out of the conversation by Val,
Phyllida watched Jake surreptitiously. He was listening

to Val telling them about the conditions in the Bass Strait, his head slightly bent as he swirled the wine in his glass, his expression absorbed. Phyllida's eyes drifted over his face, noting the rough, tantalising texture of his skin, and the way the brown hair grew at his temple. Her fingers tingled as she imagined how it would feel if she traced the line of his jaw, and she winced at the sudden, sharp ache of desire.

As if catching her expression, Jake lifted his eyes and looked across at Phyllida, with dark green eyes that seemed to reach right inside her and squeeze her heart. It was a physical effort to look away, but she managed it somehow, only to find Val—who had realised that she had lost Jake's attention—regarding her with hostility. Phyllida smiled blandly at her and, turning deliberately to Rod, monopolised his attention for the rest of the evening.

Rod, it appeared, was the only one who enjoyed himself. He made no secret of his admiration for Phyllida, and the more he flattered her the more she responded, and the more thunderous Jake looked. Val tossed her blonde hair and tried to turn the conversation back to sailing, but Rod was riveted by Phyllida, and in the end she and Jake had to resort to a low-voiced conversation together. Phyllida told herself that that was exactly what she had wanted.

Rod left with his party the following afternoon, and by tacit agreement Phyllida and Jake spent the next few days avoiding each other as much as possible. Jake went out in the evenings. He never said where he went, but Phyllida imagined him with Val, telling each other interminable sailing stories and laughing at silly little Phyllida, who didn't know one end of a boat from another and couldn't even tie a knot.

She felt unaccountably depressed on these evenings alone, and even the news from Chris that Mike was on the mend failed to cheer her up. Chris thought they would be home in about a fortnight, when Phyllida could start her holiday. No more cooking, Chris assured her. No more cleaning. Her time would be her own again.

Phyllida tried to sound enthusiastic, but when she had put the receiver down, she stood and stared bleakly at the phone. No more cleaning meant no more days down at the marina.

No more Jake.

For want of anything better to do, she had taken to spending her evenings in the kitchen, preparing extra quantities of casseroles to put in the freezer ready for the next rush. At least it stopped her sitting on the veranda, wondering where Jake was and trying to forget the way he had kissed her. While she waited for the casseroles to cook she would sit at the kitchen table with her sailing book in front of her and practise knots by tying a piece of kitchen string to the back of another chair.

She was tackling a slip-hitch one evening when Jake walked into the kitchen. He had spent the day in Adelaide and was still wearing his city clothes, with their impeccable cut and restrained good taste, reminding Phyllida of their first meeting. She had got used to seeing him in the faded shirts he wore at the marina, and it was a shock to remember that he was still a wealthy and sophisticated businessman.

Hastily Phyllida shoved the sailing book below a magazine of recipes and got up to stir the casseroles. 'You're back early,' she said a little breathlessly, wishing she could get used to the way the air squeezed from her lungs whenever she saw him. Surely she ought to be getting used to him by now? 'I wasn't expecting you until later.'

'I didn't have any English girls with enormous cases to deal with this time,' said Jake. 'It made the whole trip much easier!'

Phyllida's chin lifted instinctively. 'It sounds very dull.'

'Funnily enough, the plane *did* seem quite empty without you,' said Jake, almost reluctantly. Pulling out a chair, he loosened his tie as he sat down. He looked at Phyllida, still in her apron, and frowned. 'You shouldn't be spending all your evenings working as well, Phyllida. Things aren't so busy now.'

'I don't mind,' she said quickly, wondering if she had heard right. Had Jake actually *missed* her? 'I'm cooking some things for the freezer, so that Chris doesn't have so much to do when she comes back.'

'I see.' He hesitated. 'Does she have any idea when Mike will be able to leave hospital?'

'A couple of weeks, she hopes. She rang tonight.'

'Two weeks?' Jake seemed to hear the flat note in his voice, for he made an effort to sound more positive. 'That's excellent news.'

'Yes,' said Phyllida bleakly.

'You'll be looking forward to starting your holiday.'

'Yes,' she said again.

There was an awkward pause. Jake looked as if he was about to say something, then changed his mind. He lifted the piece of string hanging off the back of the chair instead. 'What's this?'

'Oh, nothing,' said Phyllida, coming back to the table to remove the sailing book before he saw it. But she was too late. Jake had lifted the magazine incuriously and discovered the book beneath it. He pulled it out and studied the front cover, the corner of his mouth twitching as he looked up.

'Doing your homework?'

'I just thought I'd try and master a few knots,' she said a shade sulkily.

Jake looked at the string again. 'What's this supposed to be?'

'A slip-hitch.'

The twitch became a grin, and Phyllida felt her stomach turn over at his smile. 'Don't tell me this tangle's supposed to be a slip-hitch?'

'I get confused,' Phyllida complained. 'The instructions are so complicated, I can't make head or tail of them.'

'Obviously not,' said Jake, with another pained look at the piece of string. 'A slip-hitch is simplicity itself. Come here, I'll show you.' He began disentangling the string. 'Come on,' he said again, as Phyllida hesitated.

She sat down next to him rather nervously, moving her chair so that her knee didn't touch his, and watched as he demonstrated. 'Look...round, under and through here,' he said, but Phyllida wasn't concentrating. She was looking at his fingers, so deft and sure, and remembering how they had felt against her face, against her thigh, sliding over her silken skin. 'There. Easy, isn't it?'

Phyllida swallowed and nodded.

'You have a go.' He handed her the string and she took it helplessly. Her mind was a blank, wiped clean by a terrible wash of desire that left her incapable of thinking about anything other than the strong brown hands on the table next to hers. She fumbled with the string, but got in such a muddle that Jake clicked his tongue in exasperation and pulled it away from her.

'What a mess!' he said, untying the hopelessly complicated knot she had made. 'Here, start again.'

This time he guided her fingers with his own. Phyllida felt them brush against her hands like a series of tiny electric shocks, and fought to control her breathing. It took an immense effort to focus on the string, but his hands danced before her eyes in unnatural detail. She could see every line, every hair, every pore on the tanned skin.

'I see,' she gasped when he had patiently led her through every step.

To her relief, Jake sat back. 'Knots won't mean much until you're on a boat and can practise using them. It's time I took you for a sail. How would you like to go out on the *Ali B* for a couple of days?'

'I thought you were too busy?' said Phyllida, remembering how he had poured cold water on Rod's suggestion.

'That was last week,' said Jake, not quite meeting her eyes. 'There are no boats due in or out for the next few days, and I can just as easily do the radio sched from the *Ali B*, so it seems a good opportunity. After all, I did promise Chris when I spoke to her on the phone that I'd look after you.' He glanced at her, a disturbing smile glimmering at the back of his eyes. 'Not that you need looking after, of course,' he remembered.

'No,' she said, but she didn't sound quite as definite as she had before. Appalled at the suspiciously wistful note in her voice, Phyllida caught herself up firmly. 'But I would love to go for a sail…as long as you don't think I'll get in the way.'

'Not if you do as you're told,' said Jake, getting to his feet. 'And that shouldn't be too hard—even for you!'

Phyllida stood on the jetty and hugged her jacket about her. The sky was so blue and bright that it hurt her eyes, but the wind was whipping her hair around her face, and rattling the rigging as Jake loaded the eskies onto the boat. Out on the water, yachts in full sail were heeling over at what seemed to Phyllida an alarming angle. Suddenly she wasn't so keen on the idea.

'Why don't I stay here and man the office?' she suggested as Jake emerged up the companionway.

'I thought you wanted to learn to sail?'

Phyllida cast another look at the heeling boats. 'I've just remembered that I'm not an outdoor girl,' she said. 'Are you sure it's going to be safe? It looks awfully windy.'

'Windy? Nonsense.' Jake held out an imperative hand and she climbed reluctantly on board. 'It's a nice stiff breeze—perfect sailing conditions, in fact.'

'What if I'm seasick?' asked Phyllida, perching nervously in the cockpit.

Jake was predictably unsympathetic at the prospect. 'If you're going to be sick, make sure you do it over the right side of the boat,' he said briskly, and started the engine.

He manoeuvred the *Ali B* away from its moorings with a characteristic lack of fuss, and Phyllida sat feeling hopelessly inadequate as he coiled ropes, unlashed sails and released the boom—all without appearing to be distracted from the business of steering out through windsurfers and waterskiers and fishing dinghies, not to mention small sailing boats and motor cruisers and other yachts. Phyllida kept squeezing her eyes shut and waiting for the collision, but Jake just steered calmly on, completely in control of his craft.

Once out of the sheltered waters, the wind was even stronger. Jake told Phyllida how to raise the mainsail and the jib, which she managed with much grumbling and puffing after Jake held the end of the sheet steady in one strong hand. 'I'm not strong enough,' she complained, collapsing back down next to him and clutching onto the guard rail as the wind caught the sails and sent the boat creaming through the water.

Jake glanced down at her. The shiny nut-brown hair was tangling in the breeze, and her face was pink with exertion, but her eyes were bright and wide. 'You'll get used to it,' he assured her slowly.

The next lesson was less successful. Phyllida was ordered to let out the jib sheet.

'Why?' she asked.

'Because I want to go about.'

She looked at the empty water ahead of them. 'Go about what?'

Jake sighed. 'I want to turn and tack in the opposite direction.'

'What's wrong with the way we're going?' said Phyllida.

'This is a boat, Phyllida, not a committee meeting,' snapped Jake, exasperated. 'On a boat the skipper makes the decisions and the crew—that's you—obeys his commands without question.'

'That's doesn't seem very fair! How come the crew don't get any say in what's going on?'

'Because by the time everyone's had their say, the boat's usually on the rocks! In an emergency, I don't have time to ask how you'd feel about the boom swinging towards you and knocking you off the boat, or if you'd mind terribly going about because we're about to run into a tanker, so if you want to sail you'd better learn to react quickly to orders.'

'I'd have joined the army if I'd wanted to be bossed about,' Phyllida grumbled, but she let off the jib sheet as he said.

The jib flapped frantically in the wind as Jake swung the boat round, then shouted at her to pull it in the other side. Phyllida blundered around the cockpit, dropping the hand-winch in her haste and straining frantically to pull in the sheet, but after they had repeated the manoeuvre a few times she began to get used to it, and even to feel quite proud of herself—although Jake was unimpressed.

'It's like having a baby elephant on board!' he complained as she stumbled and fell against him yet again, managing to tread on his foot this time as she hauled herself upright.

'I'm not used to operating at a forty-five-degree angle,' Phyllida pointed out, wriggling back into her position beside him, with one arm hooked around the winch and a hand clutching the guard rail for support. Jake's legs were long enough to brace himself against the other side of the cockpit, but hers could only dangle uselessly into the gap.

They had left Boston Island behind them and had settled into a long reach. The *Ali B* slid effortlessly through the waves, her bow rising and falling with the swell, and sending curves of white foam shushing and dazzling over the water in her wake. The wind filled out the sails to an arc, slicing through the blue sky, and heeled the boat over so that Phyllida could sit next to Jake and look down into the heaving, inky blueness of the sea.

Her earlier nervousness had disappeared, and, far from being seasick, she felt giddy with exhilaration. Jake's relaxed, capable presence was infinitely reassuring. In the bright light he was solid, sure, overwhelmingly distinct.

The top half of his face was shaded by a cap, but Phyllida's eye kept catching the set of his jaw and the cool, curling mouth. She had been conscious of the same sense of competence in the way he drove a car or flew a plane, but here, with his eyes screwed up against the glare, one hand controlling the yacht as she sliced through the water and the free breeze in his face, he was in his element.

He looked happy, Phyllida realised with something of a shock, as if this was where he belonged, with the sea and the sky and the bright, bright air.

Where did she belong? Doubt touched Phyllida like a cloud passing over the sun. She was a city girl, wasn't she? She belonged in the bustle of the streets, in wine bars and galleries and welcoming sitting-rooms, securely protected from the elements.

Why, then, did she feel as if she had never been so completely happy before? Ever since she had pulled Chris's photograph out of the Christmas card the idea of the sea had tugged insistently at her mind, and here she was at last.

The sun glittered on the water and flashed off the guard rails and the wind stung her cheeks, blowing away all her doubts and confusion and leaving her feeling free and invigorated, content to forget about the past and the future and live simply for this moment, with the rustling sound of the waves against the hull and the deep blue water spangled with sunshine and the diamond-bright light all around them.

A bigger wave sent up a spray of foam, and Phyllida felt the tingle of salt water against her skin. Hooking her arm more firmly round the winch, she smiled at Jake with the sunshine in her eyes, and he smiled slowly back. She watched the crease deepen in his cheek, the heart-stopping curve of his mouth and the flash of his white teeth, and sheer joy went fizzing along her veins like champagne.

'Look,' he said, and pointed. A dolphin was curving and rolling through the waves beside them, playing in the blue-white froth of their wake.

Thrilled, Phyllida craned her neck to watch his sleek grey back dive and surface, with a flash of a bright eye and the absurd smiling mouth, and then there were dolphins all around them, curious about the boat, leaping and twisting and tumbling among the waves, seeming to flow through the water with effortless speed, crisscrossing the bow to spin slowly through the sparkling blueness with their smiles and their infectious, uninhibited delight.

Phyllida felt as if she had been given an unexpected present. There was something magical about the dolphins, something inexpressibly moving about their grace and joy, and when at last they disappeared, as suddenly as they had come, they left some of their enchantment behind them like a benediction. For Phyllida, they set the seal on a day of shimmering happiness.

The wind had died to a soft breeze by the time they anchored in an empty bay off Reevesby Island. One of the largest of the Sir Joseph Banks Group, it was a long, low sandy island, barely breaking the line of the horizon, with a dazzling white beach curved around the pale green shallows. The *Ali B* was anchored in deeper waters, where the deep turquoise-blue was broken by a patch of crystal-clear apple-green above a sandy hole.

Jake tied a canopy over the boom for shade, tipped a straw hat over his face for good measure, and threw a fishing line over the side.

He had an incredible capacity for stillness, Phyllida thought enviously. She had been so busy over the last month that she felt as if she had forgotten how to sit still, and for a while she fidgeted around, picking up a book, putting it down, getting herself a drink, starting a letter but unable to get much beyond the date and 'Dear'.

She couldn't even decide who to write to. Friends at home were vague, remote figures. They would be struggling through the traffic, collars turned up against the wind and the rain, hurrying from one place to the next, and here she was, at the end of January, with the sun on her back and the silence broken only by the faint slap of the water against the hull or the plaintive cry of the Pacific gull that bobbed nearby, hoping for scraps from Jake's fishing line.

In the end, Phyllida decided to paint her toenails a deep red. Tongue caught between her teeth in concentration, she was applying varnish very carefully when something made her look up. Jake was watching her with a mixture of bafflement, amusement and irritation and something else—something that made her heart start thumping and thudding against her ribs.

'What's the matter?' she asked, annoyed at her own breathlessness.

'Nothing,' said Jake, turning away. 'Nothing.'

It might have been nothing, but Phyllida's hand was so unsteady as she returned to her nails that she daubed nail polish all over her big toe.

Gradually, though, her tension unwound in the hot peace of the afternoon. When her toenails had dried she left her book and her magazine and her writing pad behind and lay back on the for'ard deck, doing nothing, just feeling the sun on her skin and listening to the breeze sighing over the shallows. Every now and then it would catch the rigging, and the whole boat would hum like a spaceship, but mostly it rocked gently, and the light threw wavering reflections up from the water onto the white hull.

When Phyllida looked up, the rigging bisected the sky into straight lines and shapes; if she turned her head to the side, the guard rails blocked off the sea into rec-

tangles of blue and green, and behind her Jake was a
solid figure in the shade, outlined against the light.

Later he went below, and she could hear him talking
to the other Sailaway boats on the radio sched. His voice
was a deep rumble that seemed to vibrate through the
fibreglass deck and along Phyllida's skin. Opening her
eyes, she looked up at the mast soaring above her head
and let his voice drift over her body, and unconsciously
her toes started to curl.

'Now that you've discovered how to relax, it looks as
if you're doing it with your usual excess,' said Jake from
the hatchway when the radio sched was over.

Phyllida sat up reluctantly, and twisted round to face
him across the cabin roof. The dry tone wasn't matched
by the glinting humour in his eyes, and the crease in his
cheek was deepening in the way that always made her
heart turn over.

The breeze had died completely, and for the first time
she noticed that the sun had lost its glare as the day slid
imperceptibly into evening. 'Come and stretch your legs
on the beach,' he invited, and then made it impossible
to refuse by smiling.

Phyllida pulled a T-shirt over her swimming costume.
As she left her cabin she caught sight of herself in the
round mirror that hung above the locker. Her hair was
tousled, her T-shirt faded, but her face was glowing with
happiness, and, deep inside, a strange anticipation
fluttered.

Anticipation? She grimaced at her reflection. Jake had
only invited her for a walk on the beach!

'Careful,' she warned herself severely aloud. 'This is
a man who despises everything you stand for, a man
who represents everything you most dislike. He's been
rude and obnoxious and downright disagreeable, and
when Chris and Mike come back not only will you never

see him again, but you'll be glad. You're going for a walk, not a romantic tryst, so wipe that silly smile off your face and remember how much you dislike him.'

Phyllida frowned dutifully at her reflection, but her eyes were shining, and as she climbed up the companionway to Jake her unreliable, unpredictable heart began to sing.

CHAPTER SEVEN

JAKE was waiting in the inflatable dinghy that was tied to the stern. He looked up at her from where he sat by the outboard motor and smiled, and the light bounced off the water and flickered over his face. Phyllida felt her bones dissolve.

'Careful!' he said astringently as she clutched at the guard rail. 'Climb down slowly, and whatever you do don't jump, or we'll both be in the water.' Edging forward, he stood up cautiously to help Phyllida clamber down into the dinghy.

She wasn't doing too badly until he took her hand, and reaction jerked through her, making her stumble. She would have tipped right over the side if Jake hadn't caught her round the waist and held her steady as the boat rocked wildly beneath their feet.

'Talk about clumsy!' he said, but his eyes were warm and smiling, and Phyllida found herself smiling back at him. She was excruciatingly conscious of the hard hands holding her so securely, but made no move to step back. He was very close. She could see the creases at the edge of his eyes, and the dark hairs at the open neck of his shirt, and a gust of stomach-churning desire hit her just as a wave slopped against the dinghy and threatened to tip them both over.

Laughing, they sat down abruptly. Jake pulled the cord to start the little outboard motor and Phyllida was left to wonder whether it was her imagination or had he really been about to draw her towards him before that wave brought them both back to the precariousness of their

116

position? Her sides throbbed where she could swear his hands had tightened against her, and the thought sent a deep, treacherous pulse of excitement racing through her.

You're not supposed to even like him, she reminded herself, but as they pulled the dinghy up onto the shore and walked barefoot along the beach it was impossible to remember why. The light was a soft, silvery shade of purple, and the waves rippled quietly to and fro over the gleaming wet sand.

They climbed up the low dunes covered in sparse, tussocky grass, and when Phyllida looked back she could see only her own footprints next to Jake's. They might have been the first people ever to land here. The *Ali B* rocked slowly at her anchor in the deep turquoise water, and the rubber dinghy made a bright splash of colour on the beach, but otherwise there was no sign of man, only the birds skittering backwards and forwards with the waves on the shore and the vast sky stretching around them in every direction.

Later, Phyllida couldn't remember what she and Jake had talked about as they strolled around the bay on that still, silver evening.

They walked a little apart, not touching. Phyllida felt the magic of the air tangling her into a knot of awareness; she could feel every grain of sand beneath her feet, and every time Jake turned his head or smiled or lifted his hand something tightened around her heart.

The sun sank below the horizon as they headed back to the *Ali B*. They sat out on deck and watched the sky deepen from milky purple to deep gold, from gold to a fierce blaze of red.

'I'd like to keep this moment for ever,' Phyllida sighed, leaning back against the cabin. 'Wouldn't it be nice if we could freeze time and know that we could stay exactly as we are, without having to worry about practical things like visas and paying bills and looking for a job?'

She spoke without thinking, and Jake looked up sharply from where he was barbecuing the fish he had caught on a kettle fixed to the guard rail. 'I thought you had a job?'

'No.' Phyllida kept her gaze fixed on the sunset. 'I was a group account director with an advertising firm called Pritchard Price. I loved it,' she remembered, with a curious note in her voice. Her days at Pritchard Price seemed so remote now that it was hard to recall just why her job had meant so much to her.

'I was young for the job, but I'd worked really hard to get there, and I was good at it. Then Pritchard Price was swallowed up by a much bigger firm, and they gave my job to someone else. They said that there was a clash of interest between their existing clients and mine, and that they'd decided to rearrange the groupings. But the "rearrangement" was just giving all my clients to one of their more junior account directors, who just happened to have friends in high places and the luck to be male.'

She shrugged. 'One day I was called in and told to clear my desk there and then.'

Jake frowned. 'Why did you tell me you were on sabbatical?'

'I don't really know.' She rubbed her thumb absently over her fingernails. 'I suppose I found it hard to accept the truth. My life revolved around my job, and when I lost it, it was as if I didn't exist without it. I swore I'd find myself an even better job, and make Liedermann, Marshall & Jones regret that they'd let me go, but...

'Well, Christmas isn't a very good time to be looking for jobs. I decided to take the opportunity to come out and see Chris and work out exactly what I wanted to do next. In my own mind it *was* a sabbatical, but instead of going back to my old job I'd be changing to a new one.'

'And now?'

'Now?'

'You said that as far as you were concerned, it *was* a sabbatical. Does that mean you've changed your mind about going back to advertising?'

'I—' Jake's question seemed to open up a precipice beneath Phyllida's feet, and she felt as if she was teetering on the edge of a discovery she wasn't at all sure she wanted to make. The truth was that she had been so busy over the last few weeks that she hadn't given her career a thought. She *had* loved working for Pritchard Price, but did she really want to go back to the world of advertising?

It didn't seem nearly so important now as it had done, and yet what else was there? Phyllida thought bleakly. She couldn't stay in Australia for ever. She would have to go back when her visa ran out, and sooner or later she would have to find herself a job. All her experience was in advertising; it would be natural to end up in that field. Only weeks ago all her energies had been focused on her determination to get back; now the prospect left her feeling strangely flat.

'No, I suppose I'll be going back.'

'You don't sound very enthusiastic about it. I thought you were determined to prove yourself again?'

Phyllida pulled herself together. 'I am,' she said, and then, hearing the lack of conviction in her own voice, added in a firmer tone, 'Very determined.'

There was a pause. Jake turned the fish over on the barbecue. 'How long do you think you'll stay in Australia before you have to go back?' He sounded rather strained, and Phyllida glanced at him curiously.

'I don't know,' she admitted. She didn't want to think about leaving Australia. 'Another month, perhaps.'

'Rupert must be a very patient man,' said Jake drily. 'Is he prepared to wait until you decide to come home?'

'No,' said Phyllida, and his head jerked round from the barbecue. 'I wasn't quite honest about that either,' she confessed, not meeting his eyes. 'We were engaged, but I broke it off when I realised that I could never be the sort of wife he wanted.

'He thought I'd be happy to stay at home, warming his slippers all day. I didn't realise until I was sacked that to him my career was just a game, an affectation, something to fill in the time before I got married and became ''Rupert's wife'', without a mind or opinions of my own!'

'I find it hard to imagine that,' said Jake, with a glimmer of humour. 'Phyllida without an opinion?' He shook his head. 'No, I can't see it!'

'Rupert could,' she said bitterly. 'I'm beginning to think that all men would prefer their wives to be docile and mindless!'

Jake hooked the tongs over the side of the barbecue and sat down opposite her. 'You know that's not true,' he said, picking up his beer.

'Isn't it? Isn't that what you wanted? You didn't like being married to a successful career woman either.'

He was silent for a moment, and Phyllida wondered if she'd gone too far, but when he spoke his voice was quite even.

'I didn't mind Jonelle being successful. What I minded was the fact that, after a while, her success was all that mattered to her. You said you didn't want to be ''Rupert's wife''. Well, I can sympathise. As far as my wife was concerned, I was ''Jonelle's husband''.

'That would have been all right if she had been prepared to think of herself as "Jake's wife" occasionally,
but Jonelle never compromises. It's one of the reasons
she's so successful, but it's also the reason our marriage
fell apart. In retrospect, it's easy to see that we should
never have got married, but it wasn't so obvious at the
time.'

'Why *did* you?' Phyllida asked quietly.

Jake turned the beer bottle around and around between his hands, considering the question.

'Jonelle was—is—very beautiful. She's got long blonde
hair and green eyes and legs that go on for ever. I knew
what she was like—we'd known each other ever since
we were teenagers—but I thought we loved each other
enough for the differences between us not to matter. It
didn't take long to realise that we didn't.' He sounded
weary rather than bitter.

'Oh, it was all right at first. We lived in Sydney, and
Jonelle was working for an artists' agency. I'd never
wanted to be in the city, but my father was very ill, and
he wanted me to run the business in his stead. He'd said
it would just be temporary, and I didn't feel that I could
refuse when I saw how ill he really was.

'Jonelle liked the prestige of being associated with
Tregowan's, and she played at being hostess to increase
her contacts. She was good at her job, there's no denying
that, but the more ambitious she became, the less I saw
of her. She worked incredible hours in the office, and
if she wasn't there, she was out at some party—"net-
working" she used to call it.' He shook his head at the
memory, and took a pull of his beer.

'You must have been busy too,' Phyllida pointed out.
'Perhaps she would have been bored waiting for you to
come home.'

'That's why I encouraged her to work,' said Jake. 'I suppose if it hadn't been that she would have become obsessive about something else. As it was, I hardly ever saw her. She used to drag me along to parties, but I never really blended with her décor, and in the end she stopped asking me. It wasn't a very good time,' he remembered bleakly.

'I tried to make things work, but Jonelle's heart wasn't in it. She had her eyes set on higher things. I kept a boat on the Pittwater, and sometimes I'd persuade her to spend the weekend up there with me. I thought that if we were alone, we could get back to the way things used to be, but Jonelle didn't like sailing. She complained that it was cold and uncomfortable, and that she felt cut off without a phone or a fax.' He paused, shrugging off the memory.

'I suppose we would have drifted on for longer, but then she achieved her ambition and was offered a job in California. It was the same week my father died. Jonelle wouldn't even consider staying for the funeral. Nothing was going to stop her getting where she was going.' His smile was rather twisted.

'Even then, I tried. I was going to follow her when I'd sorted out my father's affairs, but she wrote to me from the States and told me not to bother as she'd found someone else—an American who was going to be a lot more useful to her than I ever was.'

'I...I'm sorry,' said Phyllida inadequately. She wished she had the nerve to put her arms round him. Jake's voice might have been unemotional, but Jonelle's desertion must have been a bitter blow to a man of his pride.

'Don't be,' he said. 'Just be grateful you and Rupert discovered that you wanted different things out of life before it was too late.'

Phyllida was silent, thinking about Jake rather than Rupert. It was easier to understand his hostility now. She must have seemed another Jonelle, in her smart suit and her brittle sophistication, talking about her career as if it was all that mattered to her. As it had been, she acknowledged ruefully. She had never bothered to look at her surroundings before, never stopped to smell the air or watch the way the sun cast shadows across the grass. Breaking away to Australia had taught her how much she had been missing.

She looked across at Jake. He was frowning down into his beer, absorbed in thought, but he glanced up to meet her eyes. 'Sorry, it wasn't a very edifying story, was it? Don't let it put you off marriage for good, though. It doesn't have to be like that. Look at Chris. She's got the right idea about marriage. She knows it's not easy, but she works at it. She's not constantly trying to prove herself, she's just the way she is—loyal and honest and kind.'

'She loves Mike,' said Phyllida.

'Yes, she does, and she's happy because she recognises his faults and loves him in spite—or perhaps because—of them. She doesn't expect him to be perfect.'

'I thought Rupert was perfect,' she said a little sadly. 'It didn't do me much good.'

Jake smiled. 'All or nothing?'

'Yes.' She smiled back ruefully. 'I'm afraid I'm not very good at compromises either. If I can't be utterly, completely, madly in love, then I'd rather not be in love at all.'

'Then why did you pretend that you were still engaged to Rupert when I asked you about him?'

The casual question caught Phyllida off-guard. She had tried so hard to forget that evening, but now the memory seemed to glow between them—the tautness of the atmosphere, the flare of anger, that unforgettable, devastating kiss. Was Jake remembering it too? She didn't dare look at him, didn't dare risk him reading the truth in her eyes.

She had held her engagement before her as if to ward off her own weakness. She had thought it would help her deny the attraction to Jake that held her in its coils. Much good it had done her.

She had fought it for as long as she could: she didn't want Rupert, she wanted Jake. She wanted him to take her in his arms again. She wanted to feel his mouth against her skin, his hard hands curving over her body, to let her fingers feel the flex of his muscles and drift on to explore the whole sleek, supple strength of him—

Phyllida caught her breath, aghast at the truth she had discovered in her own heart and passionately grateful for the darkness which hid her expression.

Jake was looking at her enquiringly, and with an effort she remembered the question. 'I...I... It just seemed a good idea at the time,' she said lamely.

She could see the amused disbelief on Jake's face. Did that mean he could see hers as clearly? Phyllida searched her mind frantically for a diversion. 'What brought you to Port Lincoln?' Her voice was so high and artificial that she wasn't surprised at his curious look, but to her relief he accepted the change of subject.

'After Jonelle left, there was no reason to stay in Sydney. I'd had enough of cities for a while. I've kept an interest in Tregowan's, of course, but I handed over the day to day management to my younger brother and bought myself *Ali B.*' He patted the fibreglass affectionately.

'We've been through a lot together. She's taken me round the South Pacific Islands, and all the way round Australia. For a long time I just kept moving, but when

I reached Port Lincoln, I felt ready to stay for a while. I started out with a couple of boats, and somehow the business grew and grew. I still go to Sydney regularly, and keep an eye on Tregowan's in Adelaide—hence the plane—but if I'm ever restless, I come out here. This is my real home—on deck, under the stars.'

'Don't you ever get lonely?'

Jake looked across the cockpit to where Phyllida sat, knees drawn up, arms resting on them, her skin luminous in the darkness. 'No,' he said. 'But that's not to say I never will.'

There was a long, long pause. The sea was still, the air warm and quiet, the only sound the *Ali B* creaking gently against the anchor rope. Phyllida was sure she could hear her senses twanging in the silence. Her heart slowed to a painfully sluggish beat, and she discovered that she was holding her breath. She let it out, very carefully.

She wanted to say something to shatter the sudden tension between them, but her mind was a blank, and her tongue felt dry and awkward. She stared out across the water instead, although there was nothing to see but the first faint glimmers of starlight, and every nerve was strained towards the man sitting as still and silent as the night on the other side of the cockpit.

In the end, it was Jake who broke the tension. He got up abruptly to check the fish, and announced that supper was ready. Phyllida went below to collect the salad she had made, perversely disappointed now that the atmosphere had been shattered by practicality. Before, it had been breathless, fraught with unspoken tension and an underlying current of awareness, but now it was simply strained and uncomfortable.

It was the same the next day. Phyllida had lain in the for'ard berth, staring at the closed door of her cabin and wondering what she would do if it opened and Jake came in. Her body had been beating with the desire she had fought so hard against. She'd wished she hadn't acknowledged it, wished she could go back to pretending that it didn't exist and that the hunger pulsing along her veins was no more than a bizarre chemical reaction.

But the door hadn't opened. Jake wasn't interested in *her*, Phyllida reminded herself bleakly. He was attracted to long-legged blondes, not petite brunettes—especially not a petite brunette whose one point of similarity with his beautiful wife was the very one that had caused the break-up of his marriage.

No, it would be as well not to indulge in silly dreams. Even if Jake *did* feel some attraction, what would it lead to? A few nights together? An awkward farewell? All or nothing, Phyllida remembered sadly. That was what Jake had said, and he was right.

In her heart of hearts, she knew that being a temporary diversion for Jake would not be enough. If she couldn't have all of him, she would be better off having none at all. It was all very well to wish that time would stand still, but it wouldn't. Sooner or later she would have to leave, and it would be much easier all round if she left with her heart and her pride intact.

The next morning she was polite but cool, Jake brisk in return. It was as if the warmth they had discovered walking along the beach yesterday evening had never existed. One of the other boats, moored at the other end of Reevesby, called in on the radio to say that it was having trouble with its engine, and Jake took the dinghy down to see if he could sort it out.

At first, Phyllida was glad to see him go, but it wasn't long before she began to miss his acerbic presence. Even a strained, irritable Jake was better than no Jake at all.

Unable to relax, desperate not to think about the un-welcome realisation that had kept her awake for much of the night, Phyllida sat at the table in the saloon and wrote determinedly cheerful letters home. She wrote to her parents, to her brother, to the friends who had been outraged at her treatment by Liedermann, Marshall & Jones, and last, after some hesitation, she wrote to Rupert.

Jake's story of his marriage had made her look at things from Rupert's point of view for a change, and she was sorry now for some of the hurtful things she had said. They had both been in the wrong. Phyllida didn't regret her decision to break off their engagement, but she did wish it had ended less bitterly.

It was a hard letter to write, and she screwed up several pieces of paper before she managed to get going. She was glad they had discovered in time how unsuited they were, Phyllida wrote, but she wanted him to know that she now realised that she had been thinking only about herself, and hadn't bothered to consider how he might feel. She hoped that it wasn't too late to say that she was sorry, and finished by saying that she would like it if they could continue to be friends when she came home.

Phyllida felt much better when she had finished. She was sealing the envelope when she heard the buzz of the outboard engine approaching. Hastily shoving pad and envelopes onto the deep shelf behind the seat, she climbed up on deck to find Jake tying the dinghy to the stern. Appalled at how overjoyed she was to see him again after such a short time, she forced herself to sound bright and brittle. 'Did you sort out that problem?'

'Yes,' Jake grunted, climbing on board with his usual economy of movement.

'What was wrong?'

'Do you know anything about diesel engines?'

'No,' she admitted.

'Then there's not much point in me telling you, is there?'

Phyllida's lips tightened. She was prepared to be polite, but if he wanted to be like that, let him! It just made it easier for her to reassure herself that last night's hunger and desire had been merely temporary aberrations of the mind.

They were snappy with each other as they took down the canopy and made ready to sail. Jake barked orders at Phyllida, and shouted at her if she didn't respond immediately. 'I thought you wanted to learn how to crew?' he snarled when she objected.

'Not if it means being bossed around by a frustrated sergeant major!' said Phyllida tautly. 'I'll stick to the land in future.'

'That's up to you, but in the meantime you're crew— and that means you do as I tell you!'

All in all, it was a tense sail. The breeze was flukey, gusting one minute and dying out the next, and Jake was edgy and scowling. There was no need to balance the boat today, so Phyllida pointedly sat as far away from him as possible.

The sea was in an intense, glittering turquoise, the islands streaks of white sand along the horizon, but yesterday's fizzing joy was missing. Phyllida looked in vain for the dolphins to reappear, and banish Jake's scowl with their enchantment, but it seemed as if they had abandoned her along with her happiness.

The atmosphere was so bad that she half expected Jake to suggest going back to the marina, but instead he announced gruffly that they would head south to Memory Cove, on the cape that jutted out from the mainland on the point of the Eyre Peninsula. 'Chris would expect me to take you there,' he said, as if excusing himself.

Phyllida would have preferred that he'd wanted to take her there himself, but she wouldn't admit as much, even to herself. 'Why's it called Memory Cove?' was all she asked.

'Matthew Flinders moored there in 1802,' said Jake. 'He was a great explorer and navigator, and several of the islands in the Sir Joseph Banks Group are named after places in his native Lincolnshire. He lost eight of his men when a boat overturned. Their bodies were never found, so he named the cove in their memory.'

Phyllida grimaced. 'It sounds a gloomy place.'

But when at last they anchored in Memory Cove, it was anything but gloomy. Hills covered in the dry, dusty green of eucalypts, she-oaks and pines rolled down to a beach that was a perfect curve of dazzling white sand, and where intense turquoise shallows shaded into crystal as they sighed gently against the shore. The colours were so bright, the light so sharp, that they hurt Phyllida's eyes.

Jake took her in the dinghy across the abrupt line that divided the deep blue water from the shimmeringly clear mint-green of the shallows—so clear that Phyllida swore she could see every grain of sand beneath them. He had announced that he wanted to do some maintenance on the boat, but that he would take her ashore if she wanted. Phyllida had interpreted this as meaning that he didn't want her around. Well, that was fine by her!

Standing knee-deep in the limpid water, she clutched her shoes and her book to her chest and watched rather forlornly as Jake turned the dinghy round and sped back out to the *Ali B*. She would much rather be on her own than sit around being snapped at by Jake Tregowan, she reminded herself, and, with a last wistful look, turned and waded for the shore.

For a while, she sat on the hot sand and tried to concentrate on her thriller, but her eyes kept straying back to the boat in the distance, where she could see Jake's figure moving sure-footedly around the deck. He never so much as glanced in her direction to see if she was all right, she thought crossly. Piqued, she abandoned her book, brushed the sand off her feet and put on her shoes to explore.

A rough, dusty track led inland through the rolling scrub. There had been a bush fire not so long ago, Phyllida saw. Burnt trees pointed their mutilated branches accusingly at the sun, black and silver slashes against the sky. Everything was brown or grey, or a dull, faded green, parched and bleached by the relentless heat and thrown into relief by the overpowering blue above. The sun cast broken shadows into the fine dust beneath her feet. Phyllida crushed some dessicated leaves in her fingers and bent her head to breathe in their sharp, dry fragrance.

She wished Jake were with her. The space and the silence were intimidating without him, the intensity of the light and the colours threatening to overwhelm her. Phyllida stood very still and stared down at the crushed leaves in her hand.

She loved him.

The realisation filtered slowly through her mind, and she raised her head to look blankly at a slender gum tree, its silvery trunk etched as if by a fine pencil against the light. What she felt for Jake was more than mere physical hunger. She wanted him, yes. She craved the feel of his body, the touch of his lips—but it was more than that.

She needed the reassurance of his presence, Phyllida realised with some reluctance. She, who had always prided herself on her independence, was somehow lost without him. It didn't matter whether he was smiling or shouting at her, as long as he was there she felt...*safe*. Jake was her focus, her anchor.

Her life before she met him had been a heedless rush, she saw. He had plucked her out of a whirling circle of activity that led nowhere except back to where it started, had held her between his hands and steadied her. Without him, she would be sucked back into the vortex. Phyllida felt chilled at the thought.

She walked on, without thinking about where she was going, preoccupied with her new knowledge. It had been bad enough admitting that she wanted Jake, but falling in love with him was a disaster! How had it happened? How had she got herself tangled up in this terrible web of need and desire? Panic stole into her heart. How was she going to cut herself free and face life without him?

Phyllida had no idea how long she had walked before she found herself on a headland, looking down on a wild, beautiful bay where the ocean surged onto the beach in line after line of booming surf. She watched as the waves gathered in the dark blue depths, lifted and grew until they broke in a perfect curve of glacier-green and crashed down into the maelstrom of purest, foaming white.

Life without Jake. How was she going to get through this evening, knowing that she loved him, being with him but not being able to touch him, not being able to tell him how she felt? Now, more than ever, he mustn't know.

The beach below was a sweep of pure white sand, edged by a sheer rock cliff-face on one side and the pounding surf on the other. Like her, stuck between her desire for Jake and the knowledge that he wouldn't ever need her in the same way, Phyllida thought wryly.

At first sight it looked quite inaccessible, but when she looked again she thought she could see a way down after all. And if there was a way down, there would be a way up.

Phyllida was suddenly fired with a determination to walk along the beach and climb back up again. In some obscure way, it would be a means of proving to herself that things weren't as hopeless as they seemed right now. Things might change. Jake might change; *she* might change. If she could only get to the beach, she might not have to live with this despair for ever.

Carefully, Phyllida began to make her way down. It wasn't too bad at first. The scrub caught at her bare legs, but the ground was quite solid. Gradually, though, the slope got steeper and steeper, and the dry earth started to crumble and slip beneath her shoes. Phyllida looked down and swallowed. She hadn't realised quite what a long way it was to the bottom. Perhaps this was a mistake? Perhaps she should just learn to accept loving Jake hopelessly after all?

Biting her lip, she glanced over her shoulder. It seemed as if she had come a long way, and the climb back up looked daunting from this angle. Phyllida wished she had never thought of reaching the beach. It was a stupid thing to try and do on her own anyway.

She turned a little awkwardly on the steep slope, but even as she realised the potential danger of her situation her foot skidded on the loose earth and she lost her balance. The ground dropped away so sharply that her fall gained momentum with sickening speed, and the next instant she was tumbling down through the scrub.

Terrified, Phyllida flailed out with her arms. The bushes were low and brittle here, but at last she managed to grasp one with a sturdier stem to break her fall. For what seemed an eternity, she just lay there with her face pressed into the dry soil, still clinging to the bush, her heart hammering with shock. She didn't dare look down; she didn't dare look up.

And then, miraculously, there was a shout from the top of the headland. 'Phyllida!'

'Jake!' She tried to shout back, but her voice only came out as a dry whisper.

'Don't move!' he shouted, making his way down towards her with careful, controlled ease.

Phyllida didn't think she could anyway. All she could do was lie there and wait for him.

It seemed to take for ever for Jake to reach her. Every now and then he would dislodge a shower of earth, which would rattle past her face, and she would tense, convinced that the whole headland was about to disintegrate beneath her, but at last he was there, and his strong arms went round her, holding her hard against the indescribable comfort of his body.

'Are you hurt?' he asked in a hard, urgent voice, patting her all over as if to reassure himself that she was still in one piece.

Phyllida clung to him, shaking her head into his broad shoulder. 'No. Just a bit scratched.'

'Well, that's something. Can you get up?'

Her legs were still trembling with reaction, but with Jake's arm around her, and his body as an anchor, she made it back up to the top. He was absolutely surefooted, his shoes never skidding as hers did, and his hold on her was strong and secure.

His face was set in grim, forbidding lines, but he didn't say anything until they had reached the track again, some way from the cliff-edge. Then he let her go, brushing the dust from her cheek where it had lain pressed into the ground. 'Are you sure you're all right?'

'I'm fine,' said Phyllida, but her voice quavered. She knew that she was lucky to have got off so lightly. Her shorts and T-shirt were dusty, and there were a few minor scratches on her arms and legs, but otherwise nothing to show for that terrifying tumble down the cliff.

'In that case would you like to explain what the hell you were doing down there?' She had never seen Jake so angry. He was very white about the mouth and his nostrils were pinched, the green eyes blazing with fury.

'I—I wanted to see the beach.'

'The *beach*?' he echoed incredulously, his voice rising to a shout. 'What for?'

Phyllida shook her head helplessly, which only seemed to make him even angrier.

'What was wrong with the beach you were sitting on earlier?' he demanded. 'Most people would have been quite happy with white sand and clear blue sea, but not Phyllida! No, she has to choose the most dangerously inaccessible beach she can find, and then try and break her neck getting down to it! What on earth possessed you?'

Phyllida couldn't tell him now desperate she had been at the prospect of spending her life without him. She couldn't tell him how the beach had beckoned, like a promise that things would get better, that he might, just might, learn to love her after all. 'I didn't think,' she said miserably, and Jake almost exploded.

'No, you never do, do you? You just see something you want and go straight after it, without thinking about what's involved, or who's going to have to come along and get you out of trouble! What would you have done if I hadn't seen you go over the edge? You could have been lying there for days with a broken neck before anyone found you.'

'I know, I know! I'm *sorry*!' Phyllida pressed her hands to her head. She longed to throw herself against him and cry, to feel his arms close around her and hear him tell her that he was only angry because he'd been so fearful for her, but there was no hope of that, not now.

She might as well have saved her breath. Jake was too angry to listen anyway. 'You're so full of how clever you are, and how you can look after yourself, but I can't leave you alone for five minutes! I followed you when I realised you'd gone from the beach, knowing that anything could happen once you went wandering off into the bush on your own, but I never dreamt you'd do anything as stupid as throwing yourself off the edge of a cliff!'

'I didn't throw myself off!'

'You might as well have done, and if I'd had any sense I would have left you there!' All through the long walk back, Jake kept up a diatribe about Phyllida. She was spoilt, stupid, selfish, criminally irresponsible.

Phyllida didn't say anything. He was right, anyway. She felt sick with shame at her own stupidity. She trudged beside him along the track, head down and shoulders rigid with misery, still shaken from her narrow escape, but more distressed by Jake's blistering anger and contempt. Her throat was tight, and her jaw was clenched so hard in the effort to keep back the tears that it ached, but she refused to cry in front of him.

It was an enormous relief when the grove of feathery she-oaks fringing Memory Cove appeared. Jake had run out of invective at last, but if anything his icy silence was even more terrifying than his anger. Phyllida walked unsteadily down to the shallows and scooped the blissfully cool water over her scratches, cupping it in her hands against her hot, burning face. She wanted to die.

When she lowered her hands, her eyes were huge in her white face. Damp tendrils of hair clung to her cheek and droplets of water still trembled on the end of her lashes, sparkling in the sunlight. She looked shaken and scared and very vulnerable, and when she saw that Jake was watching her she turned away, so that he wouldn't see the misery in her eyes.

The rage faded from Jake's face, and he caught her arm, pulling her back round to face him. 'Phyllida!' he said urgently. 'I didn't—'

CHAPTER EIGHT

SHE never knew what he had been about to say. There was a shout from the water, and they both jerked round to see an inflatable speeding across the shallows towards them, a big, familiar figure at the helm.

'Rod,' said Jake in a flat voice, and his hand fell from Phyllida's arm.

Rod and his party were delighted to see them, and seemed blissfully unaware that both Jake's and Phyllida's smiles were forced. They had come ashore, they said, to get the barbecue going at one of the sites that had been specially provided behind the beach, to minimise the risk of bush fires, and they urged Phyllida and Jake to join them.

There were five of them altogether, all men, and all delighted to see Phyllida. They were thoroughly enjoying their week fishing, with Rod taking responsibility for the boat, but were, they insisted, ready for some feminine company again.

The last thing Phyllida felt like was a party, but she had been dreading the evening alone with Jake even before he was so angry with her, so she smiled and agreed that it was a great idea. To her surprise, Jake was less enthusiastic. She would have thought he would have been just as anxious for some other company, but perhaps he had wanted to spend the whole evening haranguing her?

Refusing Jake's offer to take her across in the inflatable, Phyllida swam out to the boat in her T-shirt, letting the clear water wash away the dust and dirt. Its sparkling coolness soothed her scratches and her sore feelings, and by the time she had rinsed herself off with fresh water, and changed into a soft cotton shirt and cut-off trousers, she was feeling much better.

Jake had had no right to rant at her like that, she decided as she combed out her hair. All right, it had been stupid to attempt to reach the beach, but she would have been perfectly all right if her foot hadn't slipped. Anyone would think there had been a major tragedy, the way he was carrying on!

By the time they went back to the beach for the barbecue, Phyllida had talked herself into a defiant mood once more. At least this afternoon had showed her how hopeless it was even to think of Jake ever falling in love with her. Instead she knew just how much he despised her, and she was more determined than ever that he should never guess how she felt.

The other party didn't seem to notice the tension between Jake and Phyllida. They all sat on the beach in the fading light, looking out at the two boats anchored at either end of the bay. The water was still and milky pale, the sand cool and soft beneath their bare feet. Phyllida placed herself as far as possible from Jake, but made sure that he could see what a good time she was having.

She positively scintillated, laughing and flirting and trying to convince herself that she didn't care that he was ignoring her. The others were blurred figures, only Jake was clear and distinct in the dim light, and Phyllida hated the fact that she noticed every time he turned or smiled or lifted his bottle of beer to his mouth.

He was making an effort to be pleasant to a group who were, after all, his clients, but Phyllida could see a nerve beating in his cheek and sense the suppressed anger in the rigid lines of his body. In spite of her best resolutions, it made her nervous, and there was an increasing desperation to the way she laughed and chattered and exclaimed at how much she was enjoying herself.

It was late before the party broke up. Phyllida wished the others an effusive goodnight and waved defiantly as Jake ferried her, grim-faced, back to the *Ali B* on the far side of the bay.

'Wasn't that a great evening?' she asked provocatively to disguise her nerves as she climbed down the companionway. 'They're nice guys, aren't they?'

'You obviously thought so,' snapped Jake. 'Though I fail to see what's nice about a group of grown men slobbering fatuously over one girl!'

'Don't be absurd,' said Phyllida bravely. 'You were there—you could see we were just talking.'

'I would hardly describe your performance this evening as "just talking",' said Jake savagely. 'All those girlish giggles, those little sidelong looks, those tantalising smiles... I've never seen such a revolting display!'

'I'd have thought you'd have wanted me to be pleasant to your clients,' she said, tossing back her hair. '*You* certainly weren't. Haven't you ever heard of public relations?'

'The sort of relations you were promising were far from public,' sneered Jake. 'They're probably drawing lots for you even now!'

Phyllida's eyes blazed. 'How dare you?'

'You don't like the truth, do you, Phyllida? Must be your advertising background coming out! You'd rather pretend that things are the way you want them to be rather than face the facts as they really are.'

'Better than being prudish and pig-headed and prejudiced!' she flung at him. 'Well, don't worry, Jake! Chris and Mike will be back soon, and you won't have to put up with my offensive behaviour any longer!'

The muscle was still hammering away in Jake's cheek. 'Believe me, it can't come soon enough for me,' he said through clenched teeth. 'I had a pleasant, peaceful life until you arrived. Now I spend half my time wanting to shake you and the other half—' He stopped.

'Yes?' Phyllida demanded stormily.

Suddenly he was standing very close. She glared up at him, but when she saw the look in his eyes the fire and the fury in her bright face seeped away, and she began to tremble deep inside. Jake reached out and drew her to him slowly, deliberately.

'I spend the other half of my time wanting to do this,' he finished quietly, and kissed her.

The world melted around Phyllida, along with all her fine resolutions to save her pride and keep her distance. Pride counted for nothing when Jake held her against him; the future ceased to exist the moment his lips met hers. Resistance was a poor candle in the storm of feeling that swept over her as they kissed, hesitantly at first, as if half expecting the other to pull away in disgust, then with a spinning sweetness that grew into an increasing urgency.

Insistent, bewitching, his mouth explored hers, his hands moved demandingly over her curves, and Phyllida dissolved beneath his touch, gasping his name in helpless pleasure. Desire had them both in its thrall. This was no time to talk, no time to explain or wonder at the way the strain and tension of the day had led them to this point, where they clung to each other with a wild desperation, kissing and touching, half smiling, half awed by the sensations that tangled them closer and closer.

Jake's fingers were deft and sure as he peeled off first her clothes, then his own, and led her, still without words, to the wide berth with its hatch open to the moonlight. Smiling, she reached for him as he stretched out beside her, and he smiled back as he rolled her beneath him and bent to explore her silken warmth.

Phyllida shuddered with a deep, wrenching excitement at the feel of his naked body against her own, his skin against hers, the fierce hunger of his touch. It was so wonderful to be able to run her hands over that sleek, solid strength. She could feel his muscles flex and ripple beneath her fingers, and lovingly traced the bumps in his spine, dizzy with relief at being able to touch him and taste him and hold him at last.

A sigh of breeze sent the *Ali B* swinging gently on her anchor, and the sea rustled responsively against her hull, but neither Jake nor Phyllida noticed. Intent on each other, and the rhythm of love that was beating between them, they clung together, whispering endearments like secrets, murmuring breathlessly at each caress, each piercingly sweet kiss.

Phyllida was molten wax in Jake's arms, fluid desire beneath his demand, and as the urgency rolled and surged into a turbulent, unstoppable tide she dug her fingers into his back and cried out her need and her hunger.

She felt Jake smile against her breast, heard his muffled promise against her throat, and then, at last, she could welcome his hard heat and look into his eyes for one long, unforgettable moment as they paused together on the edge of time itself before the tide lifted them up and over and on together.

Caught up in the urgency of the rhythm, they let the tide carry them, plunging onwards and upwards in a frantic quest for fulfilment where there was nothing but the pulse of need and their bodies moving together in the light of the moon, and a final starburst of release and unimaginable delight.

*   *   *

Phyllida woke to the gentle creak of the boat, rocking almost imperceptibly from side to side and sending the marbled shadows that reflected up from the water wavering across the ceiling in time with the waves.

Stretching, filled with the boundless contentment of a dream, she rolled over to find Jake propped up on one elbow, watching her. The sunlight flooding the cabin made his eyes look very green, the grey flecks almost gold. For a long moment they gazed at each other wordlessly, while memories of the long, sweet night whispered over their skin.

Inexplicably shy after all they had shared, Phyllida felt faint colour tinge her cheeks and wanted to look away, but Jake's green-gold eyes held her.

'Hello,' she said.

'Hello,' said Jake, and dissolved all her awkwardness with a sudden smile. He leant over to kiss her, and Phyllida melted against him, sliding her arms around his neck and letting his possessively drifting hands snarl up all her senses again.

'Do you still want to shake me?' she murmured as she kissed his throat.

Jake smiled against her breast. 'I'm sure I will at some stage, but right at this moment I have other plans in mind!'

Satisfied, Phyllida stretched luxuriously beneath him, her fingers playing over the powerful shoulders. She loved the contrast between steely muscle and warm, sleek skin. She loved his lean, compact strength and the supple, unexpected grace in the way he moved. He was never blundering, never hurried, just slow and sure. She loved to bury her face into his throat and breathe in the scent of him, to touch her tongue to his skin and taste him, to feel his weight pressing her down into the cushions.

She loved *him*.

Awash with the enchantment of the night, Phyllida had forgotten yesterday's resolutions. She had buried the knowledge that she would have to say goodbye, ignored the fact that Jake had said nothing of how he felt. Reality meant nothing with the sunlight pouring over her and Jake's strong brown hands on her body.

Reality, though, was determined not to be dismissed that easily. Their kisses were just beginning to deepen out of control when there was a thump on the side of the boat and a voice called, 'Ahoy, there! Anyone awake in there?'

Jake stiffened in Phyllida's arms, and sighed. 'I suppose I'd better go,' he said reluctantly, dropping a last kiss on her shoulder. 'Otherwise they'll be climbing aboard to investigate!'

Phyllida stretched again and watched the reflections rock over the ceiling. She could hear Jake conferring with someone on deck, but was too lazy to listen. She wanted to lie here all day, enveloped in sunlight.

'They want us to go over to breakfast,' said Jake, reappearing fully dressed in the doorway. 'I'm afraid I couldn't think of a good reason to refuse—and your jealous swains are determined not to let you go without seeing you again!'

She coloured and laughed, remembering her desperate attempts to persuade Jake that she wasn't interested in him. Why had she bothered? she wondered happily as she pulled on shorts and a shirt and splashed cold water over her face. She had come a long way from the days of suits and full make-up.

When she emerged, glowing, from the cabin, Jake was tidying up the saloon. 'Making everything ship-shape?' she teased, and ran her hand down his back as he bent to retrieve her shirt from the floor where it had fallen unheeded last night.

He grinned as he straightened. 'Messy crew get put on short rations,' he said, handing her the shirt.

'I can't think how it got there, Captain,' said Phyllida with an innocent look. 'But I'll make sure it doesn't happen again!'

Jake laughed, and tugged at her hair. 'We don't need to take tidiness too far,' he relented with mock reluctance. 'Here,' he went on, picking up her shorts and pants and piling them into her arms, 'you'd better take these as well... And while you're at it, you can get rid of these, too.'

He reached into the shelf for the notepad and the letters she had written yesterday morning, and balanced them precariously on the top of the pile. 'They were sliding around all over the place yesterday.'

'Aye, aye, Cap'n!' Phyllida attempted a salute, dislodging the top letter from the pile. It fluttered to the floor at Jake's feet, and as he picked it up his smile faded. He handed it back to her, his expression suddenly quite blank, and she felt a cold feeling trickle down her spine.

Phyllida glanced at the envelope, and the name sprang out at her in her bold black writing: Rupert Deverell. 'I...er, wrote to Rupert,' she said uneasily, unsure of why she had to acknowledge it.

'So I see.'

'You see, I wanted to explain—'

Jake held up a hand to interrupt her. 'You don't need to explain anything, Phyllida,' he said, in the same crushingly cool voice.

'No, I meant to Rupert. I just—'

'I don't want to know,' he said flatly.

'But Jake, you don't understand!' To Phyllida's intense frustration she was interrupted again, this time by a shout from the other boat.

'Coffee's ready! Come aboard!'

Without a word, Jake turned and climbed up on deck.
In silence, they buzzed across in the dinghy to join the
others.

Phyllida couldn't believe how swiftly the atmosphere
had changed, how utterly the joy had drained from the
morning. All her doubts came rushing back. If Jake had
loved her, he wouldn't have turned cold on her like that,
with no provocation. He could hardly have made it
clearer that last night hadn't changed anything between
them.

'You look as if you're suffering a bit,' Rod said to her
sympathetically. 'Regretting all that wine last night?'

For a fleeting moment, Phyllida's eyes met Jake's. 'I'm
regretting a lot of things about last night,' she said evenly,
and Jake's face tightened as he looked away.

They left as soon as they could, in spite of urgings to
stay. Jake made some excuse about having to get back
to the marina, and Phyllida smiled brightly and agreed.
They didn't look at each other as they went back to the
Ali B, and Jake began preparing the boat to sail with a
brisk efficiency that chilled Phyllida to the bone.

It was ridiculous to let things sour so completely, she
decided. 'Look, Jake, about Rupert—' she began as he
unlashed the mainsail. But he was in no mood to listen.

'I don't want to hear about Rupert,' he said. 'Who
you write to is your affair. I'm not interested in how you
feel about your engagement or what you do when you
get back to England. It's got nothing to do with me.'

He went forward before she could answer, and began
hauling up the anchor. Sick at heart, Phyllida waited
until he came back and started the motor.

'Didn't last night mean anything to you?' she asked
quietly.

'It was great,' he said with chilling indifference. 'I'm
not going to pretend it wasn't. But it didn't change the

fact that your life's in England, Phyllida, not here. If you want to have a fling while you're away, well, that suits me fine—but a fling is all it is. I learnt my lesson with Jonelle. I don't want to be part of your life, juggled between your job and your other commitments. You can keep Rupert for that.'

'Jake, it wasn't *like* that,' Phyllida pleaded, but he only hunched a shoulder irritably.

'Let's leave it, shall we?'

Phyllida gave up. 'I don't want to be part of your life'. Well, what had she expected? That last night's breath-taking joy would be enough? That the glorious, spiral-ling passion would somehow change all the facts? Jake was right. She didn't belong here, with the wind and the wide sky. She was just having a fling.

Phyllida remembered his description bitterly. It might have been a fling for him, but for her it had been the source and the fulfilment of love. Hadn't he heard her, murmuring 'I love you' against his skin? Couldn't he read it in her eyes?

Numbly, she stared out across the waves and felt misery settle itself, cold and leaden, in the pit of her stomach.

The wind was light today, blowing from right behind them, so that Jake let the mainsail right out until it was almost at right angles to the boat. In front of it, cut off from the breeze, the jib flapped frantically, as if gasping for air.

Jake frowned. He had been sitting morosely at the helm, glancing automatically from sea to sail, checking the wind, his face closed, his mouth set grimly. Running before the wind like this, there was nothing for Phyllida to do, but she would even have welcomed some of Jake's abrupt commands to break the silence that grew tauter and tighter with every passing minute. When Jake did speak, she jumped.

'Take the helm, will you?' His voice was harsh.

Phyllida edged back and took the helm nervously. 'What are you doing?'

'I'm going for'ard to goosewing the jib. If I can pull it round, and brace it with the spinnaker pole, it'll catch the wind on this side and we'll get on a bit faster.'

'What do I have to do?'

Jake pointed to the compass. 'Just hold this course, and don't let the boat swing across the wind. OK?'

She nodded. It didn't mean much to her, but he would only bite her head off if she asked questions.

Jake unlashed the spinnaker pole and climbed out of the cockpit to make his way forward. Phyllida's gaze followed him automatically. She hadn't been able to look at him all morning, but now that his back was turned she could let her longing stare rest on the broad shoulders, the lean hips and the strong brown legs. Fatally, she took her eyes off the compass.

Preoccupied with memories, she didn't notice that her grip had slackened on the helm until the *Ali B* swung round into the wind, and the heavy boom went crashing across the boat. It caught Jake across the shoulders with a terrific blow, and would have knocked him overboard if he hadn't fallen against the guard rails where he lay ominously still.

'Jake!' Phyllida dodged the still wildly swinging boom and scrambled up beside him. 'Oh, Jake... Oh, my God... Jake, *please*, are you all right?'

For one black, terrifying moment she thought she had killed him, but he stirred and groaned, and she burst into overwrought tears. 'Jake, I'm so sorry...I didn't realise... are you hurt?' she sobbed incoherently.

With an immense effort, Jake pulled himself groggily into a sitting position and pushed her away. 'What happened?' he groaned, dropping his head into his hands.

'It was the boom ... it swung round before I could stop it.'

'I *told* you to keep the wind behind you!' Somehow Jake got himself down to the cockpit, where he collapsed on the lockers, wincing as he held his chest.

The boat had rounded up into the wind, and both sails were flapping aimlessly. 'What shall I do?' asked Phyllida in panic, looking around her wildly for another boat. If Jake was badly hurt, there was no way she would be able to sail the *Ali B* back single-handed. Never had she felt so useless.

'Don't ... touch ... anything,' Jake ground out, eyes tightly closed.

'But we're drifting!'

Jake grimaced as he dragged himself up to look around them. The sea stretched glittering off into the distance and the nearest land was miles away. 'We're not going to run into anything,' he said with difficulty and, lying down, closed his eyes once more. 'And I'd feel safer if you just sat completely still and didn't do anything!'

It was some time before he sat up again. He wouldn't even let her do anything for him, refusing to let her even touch him. Rejected, guilty, desperately worried, Phyllida sat miserably hunched in the corner and watched him grit his teeth and force himself to recover enough to take the helm again.

'Shouldn't you go and lie down below?' she asked timidly.

'And who's going to sail the boat? You?' Jake's voice was justifiably scathing. 'If I'd been knocked overboard, unconscious, I would have drowned, and you wouldn't even have been capable of turning the boat round to pick me up!'

'I'm sorry—'

Jake ignored her attempt to apologise. 'All you had to do was hold onto the helm and keep a steady course for two minutes, but you couldn't even concentrate for that long!'

'I didn't know what you meant!' said Phyllida tearfully. 'I only got on a boat for the first time two days ago, and you expect me to be Captain Cook already!'

'If you didn't understand, why didn't you ask?'

'Because you'd just have been unpleasant about it!' A mixture of guilt and relief was curdling her temper. 'How am I expected to learn, when all you ever do is shout at me?'

Later, Phyllida couldn't remember just how they got themselves back to the marina. All she knew was that she never wanted to go through another experience like it.

She was frantic with worry about Jake, who stubbornly refused any help. He was obviously in pain, but seemed to find some relief in a savage denunciation of Phyllida's character, actions and all she stood for, and by the time they finally tied up at the marina she was white with rage, shock and humiliation.

Scorning her assistance, Jake took himself off to the hospital, and Phyllida was left miserably cleaning the boat. It seemed to be all she was good for nowadays, she thought wearily. She found Jake back at the house when she had finished.

'What did the doctor say?'

'Three cracked ribs, heavy bruising and a touch of concussion,' said Jake. 'Although it feels more like a bloody great whack than a touch! He's told me to rest, so I'm going to bed.'

'Can I do anything?' she asked in a small voice.

He turned at his bedroom door. 'Yes,' he said with brutal frankness. 'You can keep out of my way for a while!'

Phyllida sank down into a chair and buried her face in her hands, letting the hot tears course down her cheeks. Only this morning he had held her and kissed her and whispered sweet words into her skin; now he was a bitter stranger again.

Her heart felt as if it was full of pebbles, scraping and rasping painfully against each other like shingle on a beach, as wave after wave of misery swept over her. Memories of last night mocked her. What a naïve fool she had been, to place such trust in love to make everything right! Love had been all that mattered last night, and now everything was wrong—terribly wrong.

She sat dully all evening, thinking about the night before, and all the lonely nights to come when all she would have would be memories of Jake's lips and Jake's hands and Jake's hard, exciting body. When the phone rang she was tempted to ignore it, but roused herself to answer listlessly.

'Phyllida?' It was Chris's voice. 'What on earth's the matter?'

'Nothing,' said Phyllida with an effort. 'I'm just tired. It's been a long day. How's Mike?' she added quickly, before Chris could pursue the subject.

'A bit wobbly, but on his feet at last. That's why I've rung: we should be home next week!'

She chattered on for a while, and Phyllida was so pleased to hear her bright and happy again that she forced herself to sound cheerful in reply. Chris wasn't fooled, though. 'Something *is* wrong, isn't it?' she said suspiciously.

Phyllida hesitated. She couldn't tell Chris about Jake. She would be distressed if she knew just how miserable Phyllida was, and anyway, her feelings for Jake were too raw and painful to talk about just yet. On the other hand, she would have to tell Chris something, or she would bully the truth out of her anyway.

'I . . . I'm missing Rupert,' she improvised.

'Rupert? But I thought you were the one who broke off the engagement?'

'Yes, I was but . . .' Phyllida trailed off helplessly, then rallied. 'I've had some time to think about things,' she said. 'I didn't realise how much I'd miss him.' None of it was true, she thought bleakly, but it didn't seem to matter. Nothing seemed to matter any more.

Chris was surprised, but so sympathetic that Phyllida began to feel guilty about misleading her. 'I didn't mean to unburden my problems on you,' she said, trying to stem the flow.

'Don't worry. It makes a nice change to worry about somebody other than Mike,' said Chris cheerfully.

Jake was stiff and surly for the next few days, snapping at Phyllida when she suggested he go back to the doctor. Hurt, wretchedly unhappy, she retreated behind a barrier of frigid hostility, and kept out of his way as he wanted.

It was impossible to avoid him completely, of course. She had to pass him in the office when she went to collect fresh linen, or edge past him on the narrow pontoons, and her heart was so sore she wanted to cry out with the need to touch him.

Jake himself spoke to her as little as possible, and, to rub salt into the wound, spent much of his time with Val, who always seemed to be around, spotting places Phyllida had missed with the polish or dealing competently with the radio.

Phyllida gritted her teeth and carried on doggedly. She didn't cry.

Alone at night she would lie in bed and stare at the ceiling, remembering how the moonlight had poured through the hatch on the *Ali B*, but even tears seemed frozen up in the cold bleakness inside her. She tried to think positively, and make plans for the future, but it was as if her world had shrunk and it was impossible to imagine a life without Jake or the cheerfully rocking boats in the marina.

Mike's progress was still satisfactory; he and Chris would be home soon. Phyllida didn't know whether she longed for this nightmare situation to end or dreaded the time when she would have to say goodbye to Jake.

Three days before Chris and Mike were expected, Phyllida was cleaning *Valli* again. She knew each boat like an old friend by now, and she would miss them as much as she would miss the huge sky and the dazzling light and the soft slap and sigh of the water against the jetty.

Gathering up the dirty sheets and pillowcases into a huge bundle, she took them along to the office. Jake was there, scowling over some accounts, and, although he didn't look round, she could tell from the stiffening of his body that he knew she was there.

Phyllida looked at the back of his head and wished that she could slip her arms around his neck and bend down and whisper 'I love you' in his ear. She wished he would turn his head and smile, and pull her into his lap so that she could kiss the lines of strain from his face...

What was the point in wishing? Phyllida remembered bleakly. Wishing hadn't made things right before. So, instead of putting them around Jake, she tightened her arms around her bundle of dirty washing and headed into the back room, where she dumped them in the basket and began pulling out clean sheets from the store.

In the other room, she heard the creak of Jake's chair as he swung round the way he did when someone came to the door of the office. 'Can I help you?' His voice was preoccupied, not overly welcoming.

There was a murmur, and then Phyllida heard him call her name. Puzzled, she went to the door, her arms full of sheets which went cascading to the floor as she saw who was standing in the office waiting for her.

'Rupert!'

CHAPTER NINE

RUPERT smiled. Next to Jake he looked cool and pale and patrician, and somehow insubstantial. 'Phyllida, darling!' he said.

Jake looked from Rupert's handsome face to Phyllida's stunned expression, and his face hardened. 'This is obviously a personal call,' he said coldly.

'It is,' said Rupert smugly. 'Very personal.' He turned back to Phyllida. 'Is there somewhere we can be alone, darling?'

Her eyes flicked helplessly to Jake, who was looking thunderous. His chair scraped across the floor as he got to his feet. 'You can stay here,' he said curtly. 'But don't be too long. Phyllida's got a lot to do, and I don't pay her to stand around gossiping all day.'

Rupert glanced at him with ill-concealed dislike. 'We've got better things to do than gossip,' he said. 'I haven't seen Phyllida for more than two months, and we've got a lot to talk about.'

'In that case, I suggest you talk about it in her time, not mine,' said Jake. 'You can have five minutes now, but otherwise you'll have to postpone your touching reunion until Phyllida's finished work.' He looked stonily at Phyllida. 'I'll be on *Calypso* if anyone needs me.'

I do, Phyllida wanted to cry after him. She watched him walk out of the office and along the jetty, his stiffness almost gone, and it seemed as if he was walking out of her life without a backward look.

154

'He's a bit grim, isn't he?' said Rupert, shutting the door after Jake. 'How on earth do you come to be working for a rough type like that?'

'It's a long story.' Blankly, she bent to pick up the sheets she had dropped, and clutched them to her chest as she faced Rupert. His image had become blurred in her mind over the last few weeks, but she could see now that he was just the same.

His hair was the same dark gold she had once loved, his eyes the same blue, and there was the same faint arrogance in his expression. He had been the best looking man she had ever met. He still was, Phyllida considered fairly, but he didn't make her heart leap or her senses tingle just by standing there, like Jake did.

'This is a surprise,' she said with an effort. She felt oddly disorientated by his sudden appearance. 'How on earth did you find me?'

Rupert looked rather taken aback, as if he had expected her to throw herself into his arms. 'I've just flown out from London,' he said. 'I thought you'd be at your cousin's address, but when I got there a neighbour said I'd probably find you at the marina. So—' he smiled and spread his hands '—here I am.'

'You always used to be so rude about Australia,' said Phyllida, putting the sheets down on a chair with an awkward laugh. Once, when they had just got engaged, she had suggested that they come out together, so that she could introduce Rupert to Chris, but he had poured scorn on the idea, saying that it was a barbaric country and that he had better things to do with his holiday than stand around in a lot of dust, photographing kangaroos. 'Don't tell me you're out here on business?'

'Personal business,' said Rupert, walking towards her and taking her hands. 'I came to find *you*, Phyllida. I want you to come home. I was angry after that awful argument, but after you left I realised how much I missed you. I've been thinking about things, and I know that I should have been more sympathetic when you lost your job. I realise now how much it meant to you, and if you want to go on working after we're married, I won't mind—I promise.'

Phyllida stared at him in astonishment. 'You mean, you still want me to marry you?' She couldn't believe he thought it would be that easy.

'Of course I do!' Rupert put his arms round her, evidently expecting her to be speechless with joy, and he looked hurt when she wriggled free. 'What's wrong, darling?'

He wasn't Jake, that was what was wrong. Phyllida hugged her arms together in an unconsciously defensive gesture.

When she had thrown Rupert's ring back in his face, she had sworn to make him regret his lack of sympathy. Well, now he did. Her wish had come true. He had said that he loved her and understood her need for a career, just as she had longed for him to do. It should have been the perfect ending, a fairy tale come true, but all Phyllida could feel was panic at finding herself in the wrong scene, with the wrong hero.

How could she tell Rupert that? She hesitated, wanting to tell him the truth but reluctant to hurt him. He had just flown all the way from England to see her. It wasn't fair to tell him that he had wasted his time as soon as he had arrived. She should let him explain himself properly; she owed him that at least.

She glanced around the office. 'We can't discuss this here,' she temporised. 'You're tired. Why don't we talk about things when you've had a chance to sleep?'

'Of course,' said Rupert with a smile, certain that she would come round to his point of view eventually. 'I've sprung this on you without warning, haven't I? No wonder you're behaving strangely!'

It was on the tip of Phyllida's tongue to inform him sharply that there was nothing strange about *her* behaviour, but she bit back her retort. She didn't want to start an argument here.

She found Jake on *Calypso*, savagely polishing the guard rails. He looked up as she approached and wiped his hands on the rag. 'So that's Rupert!' he sneered. 'Very aristocratic! Was he offended because I forgot to tug my forelock?'

Phyllida clenched her hands. 'He didn't mention you.'

'What's he doing here, anyway?'

'I don't think that's any of your business,' she said steadily.

'Let me guess!' said Jake with bitter sarcasm as he went back to his polishing. 'He's come to sweep you out of this ghastly hovel and carry you back to the family mansion, where you can use your famous executive skills organising all the old retainers? No more cooking and cleaning for you! I can't help feeling you'll be a little bored, though, Phyllida. Rupert's not man enough for a girl like you.'

'He's man enough to apologise, which is more than you are!' said Phyllida before she could stop herself. She took a deep breath and counted to ten. 'Rupert's tired,' she went on in an even tone. 'I'm going to take him back to Chris's house so he can sleep. He's hired a car, so I might as well collect my things and go back with him.'

'Very cosy!' jeered Jake. 'Sure you'll be able to manage without a butler?'

Phyllida ignored him. 'I'll get a taxi back later this afternoon.'

'Don't bother,' he said. 'Far be it from me to wrest you from the arms of your lover, who's come so far to see you!'

'I thought things were supposed to be too busy to allow me more than five minutes off?'

Jake dug his rag into the tin of polish and attacked one of the uprights. 'The business isn't going to fall apart without you. I've managed without you before, and I'll manage again.'

Would *she* manage without *him*? 'I'll be here to-morrow morning, then.' When Jake didn't reply, or look up from the guard rails, Phyllida sighed and walked away, but when she glanced back from the end of the jetty, she saw that he had put down his rag and was staring at her.

While Rupert slept Phyllida sat out on the shaded veranda and watched some pink and grey galahs settle with a lot of squawking and fussing in the tall gum tree across the road. She had managed to persuade him that she needed time to think, and he had agreed not to press her for an answer yet.

She *did* need to think, she told herself. She had been wrong before; might she not be wrong again? Perhaps Jake was right, and this *was* just a temporary madness that would fade as soon as she got back into her old routine. She ought, in fairness, to give Rupert the chance to remind her about the things that had once been so important to her.

Phyllida had cleared out the fridge before she went to Jake's, so they had to go out to eat. Knowing how snobbish Rupert could be, she took him to the best res-taurant in town, but found herself wincing at his car-rying cut-glass tones and patronising glances.

'Liedermann, Marshall & Jones have been asking round about you,' he told Phyllida when they had ordered. 'Rumour has it that they want you back. In fact, Barry Shillingworth asked me to tell you to get in touch as soon as you got back.' He reached out and covered her hand with his own. 'You see, darling, we all want you!'

Jake didn't, Phyllida thought wistfully. Tugging her hand away as unobtrusively as she could, she looked desperately over Rupert's shoulder in search of a diversion, only to find herself staring into familiar green, grey-flecked eyes.

Phyllida felt jarred and breathless, as if she had tripped at the unexpected end of an escalator, or missed the last step on the stairs. For a shocked moment she wondered if her thoughts had conjured him up out of thin air, and then she saw that he was with Val, and that they were already embarked on their meal.

So this was where he brought her! Sick with jealousy, Phyllida looked defiantly back at Jake over Rupert's shoulder. Her eyes were bright and hostile, his cold and accusing.

'Well, I must say you don't look very enthusiastic,' Rupert was complaining, and with difficulty she brought her attention back to him. 'I thought you'd be over the moon! You always used to be obsessed with that damned job of yours.'

'I'm sorry, Rupert.' Phyllida shrugged her shoulders helplessly. He was right. She should be ecstatic at the idea of having her old job back. 'I suppose it's all happened too quickly. It's going to take some getting used to.'

'I don't see why,' he said a little sulkily. 'It's not as if you have to think about anything new. It'll just be going back to exactly the way you were before. I thought that's what you wanted.'

'I've had a lot of time to think since I came to Australia,' she tried to explain. 'Don't you see? I can't just pretend that LMJ never sacked me, or that we never had that argument!'

Rupert looked at her in disbelief. 'You won't get another chance like this, Phyllida. The way Barry was talking, you might even be up for a promotion if you go back now. You never used to be slow about taking opportunities to get on!'

'No,' she admitted ruefully. 'I know I built my life around my job. But now that I've had a chance to stand back and think about things, I don't know if I want to go back to advertising.'

His face lit up. 'You mean, you don't want to work after all? We can get married as soon as we get back, then!'

'I didn't mean that,' said Phyllida quickly, before he got carried away. 'I'm just not sure what I want at the moment.'

'You've changed,' said Rupert, staring at her as if he'd never seen her before, and, over his shoulder, Phyllida's eyes met Jake's unwillingly once more.

'Yes,' she said. 'I have.'

Rupert was happy to accept her change of heart about her career, but refused to believe that she wasn't just being coy in refusing to give him a direct answer. 'We could be on our way home in a couple of days!' he pointed out. 'There's nothing to keep you here now that you've made your point.'

'This isn't a game,' said Phyllida wearily. 'Let me sleep on it, Rupert. I don't want to rush into another decision.'

The meal seemed to last for ever. Phyllida tried everything to keep her gaze on Rupert, but her eyes kept sliding over his shoulder and jarring with Jake's with such a clash that she half expected Rupert and Val to twist round in their chairs and demand to know what all the noise was.

All in all, it was a relief when Jake and Val got up to go. Phyllida relaxed back in her chair, only to jerk upright when she realised that they would have to pass the table on their way out.

Val stopped in surprise at the sight of Phyllida. 'Hello! I didn't know you were here.'

'Small world,' said Phyllida with a brief smile. She glanced at Jake. 'Hello,' she said coolly, as if they hadn't been glaring at each other for the last hour.

'This is Phyllida's fiancé,' said Jake, managing to turn the description into a sneer. 'It's Rupert, isn't it?'

'Rupert Deverell.' Rupert looked as if he didn't know whether to be pleased at Jake's description or offended by his tone.

'I'd have thought you two would have wanted to be alone tonight,' Jake went on nastily. 'Surely the reconciliation's not over already?'

'Of course not,' said Rupert, looking down his nose. 'One must eat.'

'If I hadn't seen my fiancé for over two months, food would be the last thing on *my* mind!' said Jake. 'But then, if I had a fiancé—especially one like Phyllida—I wouldn't let her go away for months on end.'

Rupert half rose from his seat. 'What do you mean by that?' he demanded angrily.

'He means that he hasn't got a fiancée because no girl would ever consider marrying anyone with his kind of suspicious and possessive attitude,' said Phyllida, with a vengeful look at Jake as she pulled Rupert back into his chair where he subsided, muttering.

'I didn't know you were engaged, Phyllida,' Val put in quickly, before the argument could develop any further.

'Didn't you?' Phyllida glanced at Jake in frustration. Why had he called Rupert her fiancé? She had told him the truth at Reevesby Island, but she could hardly deny it in front of Rupert before she had had a chance to tell him in private that she wasn't going to change her mind.

'If I'd known you were here, I'd have asked you and your fiancé to join us,' Val went on, running her hands through her blonde mane. 'We've been planning a round-the-world trip and could have done with your culinary advice—neither of us know the first thing about cooking, do we, Jake?'

Phyllida felt as if she had been struck. Jake and Val, planning a round-the-world trip together? Jake and Val, lying together night after night in the for'ard berth, with the stars shining down on them? Jake and Val, strolling along empty beaches in the still evening light? She wanted to stand up and scream No!, to wipe the smug smile from Val's face and tell her that Jake belonged to *her*.

Her lips were stiff, her throat tight and dry. 'I'm sure Jake will tell you that I'm no good for anything on a boat.' She looked at him, daring him to remember how they had braced themselves against the side and watched the dolphins leaping through the water, how they had sat and talked while the sunset flamed and faded, how they had made love in the starlight.

Jake looked back at her, his eyes dark and angry, and she knew that he remembered only too well, and resented her for reminding him.

Rupert was laughing indulgently. 'Don't tell me you've been sailing, darling? It's obviously high time I took you home, before you become a real outdoor girl!' He put his hand over hers. 'And I like you firmly indoors—and preferably in bed!'

Jake's expression was so murderous that for one moment Phyllida thought he was going to hit Rupert, but in the end he only took Val's arm in a grip that made her wince. 'We'd better not keep you, then,' he said, his voice like a steel trap. 'You'll want to get back there as soon as possible!'

'Well!' Rupert stared after him in outrage. 'Who does that chap think he is?'

Phyllida's eyes followed Jake out of the restaurant. She had longed for him to go, and now the room felt cold and empty without him. 'He's not always like that,' she said, thinking of Jake laughing, Jake smiling, Jake whispering endearments against her skin.

'I don't know why his girlfriend puts up with him,' huffed Rupert, still much put out by the whole encounter.

His girlfriend. Val. Lucky Val, who would be able to wake up every morning in her berth and turn to find Jake there. 'I expect she thinks he's worth it,' said Phyllida quietly. It didn't matter how unpleasant Jake was, she would think so too.

'I was beginning to think there might be something going on between you two,' Rupert confessed. 'It's the way he looks at you—and at me! If looks could kill, I'd be splattered all over the wall. But if he's going round the world with that girl, I suppose he's got other interests.' He hesitated. 'There *isn't* anything going between you, is there?'

'No,' said Phyllida sadly. 'There's nothing going on.'

She took a taxi to work the next morning. 'But I'm here!' Rupert had protested, peeved, when she'd announced her intention. 'This Tregowan chap won't expect you in.'

'The boats still have to be cleaned,' Phyllida had said, although the frantic rush was over, and none of the boats going out that weekend wanted catering. 'And there's no point in my hanging around while you sleep off your jet lag. You can come and pick me up later.'

Rupert had grumbled, but she'd insisted. The marina was the only place that felt like home at the moment, and her need to be near Jake was a physical ache. There might be nothing between them any more, but she still needed to see him. It didn't matter if all she could do was watch him; knowing he was there was enough.

She had lain awake long into the night, torturing herself with thoughts of Jake and Val together. Would it have made any difference if she had known how close they were? Why had he made love to her if he had been planning to go away with Val? Phyllida's tired brain couldn't come up with any answers. All she knew was that even the dream of a future with Jake had died, along with all her other dreams.

Jake's expression was even more forbidding than usual, and he avoided Phyllida until she was putting the buckets and scrubbing brushes away at the end of the day. 'Chris rang a little while ago,' he said flatly. 'She and Mike are coming home a day early. They'll be back tomorrow.'

Tomorrow? Phyllida was overwhelmed with panic at the thought that the end might be so close. 'That's good news,' she muttered.

'I'll pick them up from the airport,' Jake went on. 'You'd better be at the house to meet them. There's no need for you to come here. We're not busy, and I can manage on my own until Chris is ready to come back.'

'I see.' She didn't even have tomorrow. The end was today. Now. Numbly, Phyllida picked up her bag. 'So this is goodbye?'

Jake got to his feet. 'I . . . yes, I suppose it is.' He hesitated, as if he wanted to say more, but when he did speak, his words were stilted and formal. 'Thank you for your help.'

'That's all right.' Phyllida's body felt as if it didn't belong to her any more. She couldn't go like this, without telling him how she felt! She swung round. 'Jake?'

'Yes?' His tone wasn't encouraging.

'Jake, I . . .' Phyllida faltered and stopped. It ought to be easy to tell him that she loved him and needed him, that her heart was breaking at the thought of never seeing him again, but the words stuck in her throat. He would laugh in her face. He would snap his fingers and tell her that she could keep her love and go back to her precious career.

Jake's eyes were suddenly alert as she hesitated. 'Well?' he prompted urgently.

Let him laugh, Phyllida decided. At least she would have told him. 'I just wanted to tell you—'

An imperious blast of the horn interrupted her. Through the window she could see Rupert at the wheel of his hired car, and her shoulders slumped. Jake's face hardened.

'You'd better go,' he said. 'You don't want to keep his lordship waiting.'

Phyllida bit her lip, then nodded. She couldn't tell him with Rupert peering through the window at them. Perhaps it wasn't meant to be. Perhaps in time she'd be glad she hadn't said anything. 'Goodbye,' she said in a low voice, and walked quickly out to the car.

Rupert was still feeling aggrieved at having been neglected all day. He complained all the way back to the house. 'I just don't see why you had to go into work,' he continued as she unlocked the door. 'It's not as if the fellow's even paying you!'

'That's not the point,' said Phyllida tiredly.

'Well, what is? He's not a charity, and I don't like the idea of my fiancée spending her days acting as an unpaid char—especially not for a man like that.'

'I'm not your fiancée,' she said, dropping her bag onto a chair and turning to face him. 'I haven't been since I gave you back your ring.'

Rupert frowned. 'I thought we'd decided we'd put all that behind us.'

'*You* decided that. I didn't.'

'Are you trying to tell me that I've come all this way for nothing?' he demanded incredulously.

She sighed. 'I was upset after that argument. Of course I was. If you'd come round to see me the next day, and told me what you told me yesterday, I'd probably have fallen into your arms and we might have been able to carry on as before. Now I'm glad that you didn't.'

'*Glad*?'

'I know now that it would have been a terrible mistake for us to get married,' she explained, as gently as she could. 'We didn't know enough about each other, Rupert. I didn't realise until that argument just how different we are.'

'We're not different,' he protested. 'We lead the same life, have the same interests, share the same friends... What's different in that?'

Phyllida looked at him helplessly. 'We think differently.'

'What nonsense!' said Rupert, with a dismissive gesture. 'Australia seems to have gone to your head. You'll soon change your mind when you're back home again.'

'I don't want to change my mind.' She took a deep breath. 'I'm sorry, Rupert. I can't marry you because I don't love you. I don't think I ever did.'

Rupert's expression clouded with gathering fury. 'Do you realise what I've given up to come running after you, Phyllida? It wasn't an easy time to leave the firm, you know. God knows what's happening while I'm not there!

'I've had a ghastly trip that's cost me an arm and a leg, I've been stuck in this benighted place for two days, and my back will probably never be the same after the most uncomfortable bed it's ever been my misfortune to sleep upon...all for you! And now you calmly turn round and tell me you won't marry me after all!'

'I didn't ask you to come,' Phyllida pointed out, annoyed by his assumption that this was somehow all her fault. 'I'm sorry you've had a wasted journey, but you could have written. I did.'

'I never had so much as a postcard from you!'

'No,' she admitted. 'I never got round to posting the letter.' She took it out of her bag and smoothed the crumpled envelope between her fingers.

Rupert was forgotten for a moment as she looked down at it and remembered how it had fallen to the cabin floor, how Jake's face had changed as he'd picked it up, how the happiness of the morning had crumbled. She hadn't changed her mind about anything she had said in the letter, but her heart had been too sore to do anything about it until now.

She handed the envelope to Rupert. 'Here, you might as well read it. It's addressed to you.'

Rupert took it with a suspicious look and ripped open the envelope. 'I see,' he said heavily when he had read it. 'So I might as well have saved myself the trip? You'd already made up your mind?'

She nodded. 'I had no idea you'd come out here.'

'Obviously not,' said Rupert bitterly. 'Why didn't you tell me all this as soon as I arrived, instead of letting me get my hopes up and make a complete fool of myself?'

Rupert hadn't just had hopes, Phyllida reflected. He had been convinced that she would fall in with his plans—just as she had always done before. She sighed. 'I'm sorry,' she said again.

'I just don't understand you,' he went on petulantly. 'I'm offering you the chance of everything you've always wanted and you turn it down! It's not as if there's anything to keep you here—this is hardly your kind of place, is it?'

Phyllida thought of the inky blue of the sea, of the sunshine dancing on the waves and the intense turquoise shallows sighing onto wide white beaches. She thought of the sky and the wind and the sound of the boat shushing through the water. And she thought of Jake, and the hard green eyes that could melt into a smile that set her heart swinging with happiness.

'I like it here,' was all she said.

Rupert snorted. 'You won't be able to stay here for ever. You know that, don't you? What are you going to do then?'

Phyllida's heart contracted. 'I don't know.'

She might have felt more guilty about Rupert if she hadn't sensed that his pride was wounded as much as his heart. He had always been fond of grand gestures, she remembered, and flying out to Australia had been the grandest of them all. Unfortunately, things hadn't worked out as he had planned, and he was not amused.

Phyllida had had her chance, he informed her petulantly, and he sincerely hoped she would live to regret it. In the meantime, he couldn't wait to shake the dust of Port Lincoln from his shoes.

All in all, Phyllida was relieved when he managed to get a place on the last flight back to Adelaide that night. He left announcing that since he had come this far he might as well do some business, visiting the vineyard in the Barossa Valley.

Phyllida hated herself for wondering cynically whether that hadn't been his intention all along, and whether coming to see her had just been a side-trip on impulse, to make the most of his ticket which he would undoubtedly manage to claim off his tax.

She spent that night alone in Chris's house, wondering whether Jake was sitting on his veranda looking out over the sea. Was he thinking about her? Did he ever remember that night they had shared? Or was he out with Val, planning their romantic round-the-world venture?

Jake's image circled round and round in her mind: Jake rolling his eyes in exasperation, Jake holding out his hand to help her onto the boat, Jake leaning down to kiss her. She tried to hold onto those memories, but darker ones kept intruding. She thought about how he had pushed her away from him, how cold and angry his eyes had been last night.

'I don't want to be part of your life.' His words echoed bitterly through her thoughts. He was part of Val's life, not hers.

It was just as well she hadn't had the chance to tell him how much she loved him, Phyllida thought bleakly. She had been so desperate at the thought of saying goodbye to him that she had forgotten Val. She couldn't have borne the thought of the two of them laughing together at the silly English girl's infatuation. How could she even have dreamt of being a rival to Val, who belonged here?

*   *   *

Phyllida was up early the next morning. She had slept
badly, disturbed by dreams of Jake drawing her towards
him with a smile only to thrust her aside in disgust when
he realised at the last moment that she wasn't Val. Misery
felt like a great weight pressing down on her shoulders
and Phyllida found that she was moving stiffly like an
old woman as she cleaned the house and made everything look nice for Chris and Mike's return.

She was just placing a vase of agapanthus lilies on the
table when she heard a car draw up outside. Her hands
shook as she set the vase down. Jake would be there.
She would have to greet him coolly, as if nothing had
happened between them. Nothing must spoil Chris and
Mike's homecoming.

Taking a deep breath, Phyllida went to the door. She
saw Jake first of all. He was helping Mike out of the
car and onto his crutches, but he looked up as the door
opened and his eyes met Phyllida's along the length of
the veranda. His expression was intense, searching, and,
without thinking, Phyllida took a step towards him.

The next instant Chris had emerged round the back
of the car and rushed towards Phyllida with a cry of
delight, enveloping her in a hug. 'You look so different!' she exclaimed, holding Phyllida at arm's length
to study her properly. 'I can't put my finger on
it...maybe it's because you've been out in the sun? Or
have you changed your hair? No, it's something else...'

Phyllida looked at her cousin in some dismay. It was
just like Chris to spot the truth at once! She forced a
laugh. 'I haven't had time to dry my hair properly, but
otherwise I'm just the same, I promise you!'

She moved forward to greet Mike with a smile, carefully avoiding Jake's eye. Mike was a tall, lanky man,
and was having trouble manoeuvring his crutches, but
he kissed Phyllida warmly and thanked her for taking

Chris's place at work. 'It made all the difference to her not having to worry about her job,' he told her gratefully.

'Won't you come in, Jake?' Chris pleaded, obviously continuing a conversation that had begun in the car. 'We haven't had time to thank *you* yet.'

'No, I won't stay,' Jake said with a brief smile. 'You'll want to settle in, and besides, this should be a family occasion. Phyllida has some news for you about Rupert.' And he got back into the car and reversed out of the drive without waiting to see what the reaction would be.

CHAPTER TEN

'WHAT on earth did he mean by that?' Mystified, Chris looked after Jake as he drove away. 'And what's all this about Rupert?' she added to Phyllida.

'Nothing important,' said Phyllida hastily. 'I'll tell you later.' She bent to pick up one of the cases. 'Come on, let's go inside.'

It was some time before they were settled with a celebratory drink under the pergola in the back garden. Phyllida was careful to steer the conversation away from what she had been doing, and for a while they were happy to tell her about Mike's stay in the hospital and how kind everyone had been to Chris.

'I did a lot of thinking when I was lying in that bed,' Mike said. 'I realised a lot of things I wished I'd realised sooner—like how selfish it was of me to drag Chris around from place to place, and how all my schemes fell through because I lost interest before they had a chance to work.' He covered Chris's hand with his own and smiled at his wife. 'That's all changed now, hasn't it?'

Chris nodded happily. 'We had a long talk one day,' she told Phyllida. 'We've decided to start afresh, but this time we're going to work together to make a real success of it. Mike found a small charter company in the Whitsundays whose owner wants to sell up, so we're going to sell our house here and use what's left of the money Jake paid us to start again. We're going to go upmarket, like Jake has, and although things will be tight at first, we're determined to make it work.'

'That's right,' Mike confirmed. 'The accident sorted out all my priorities for me. I was always restless, always thinking things would be better if only I was somewhere different or doing something different. Now I know what's important—and the most important thing of all is that I've got Chris, and she's got me.'

He smiled lovingly at his wife as he spoke. They were so happy, so confident that everything would be all right as long as they were together, that Phyllida felt tears sting her eyes.

Jake would never look at her the way that Mike looked at Chris. She would never be able to smile like Chris and know that everything would be all right because Jake would always be at her side. They wouldn't share the doubts and the worries along with the laughter, or look forward to a bright future, secure in the knowledge that they would share it together.

Phyllida blinked the tears away furiously. This was no time to waste in what-might-have-beens. It was Chris's happiness that mattered now, and no one deserved it more. 'I'm so pleased for you,' she said warmly.

'Now, tell us about Rupert!' Chris commanded. 'What did Jake mean by saying that you had some news?'

'Rupert turned up here a couple of days ago,' said Phyllida, and laughed at the look on Chris's face.

'He came all the way out to Australia to see you?' she asked excitedly.

'Me and a few vineyards,' Phyllida said with a dry look.

'But Phyllida, that's wonderful news! How have you managed to keep it to yourself while we've been boring on about our news?' She paused, puzzled by her cousin's expression. 'I suppose he *did* come to beg you to go back to him?'

'He said he still wanted us to get married.' Phyllida chose her words carefully. Rupert hadn't done much begging. Assuming was more his line.

Chris was looking bewildered by Phyllida's restrained manner. 'Isn't that what you wanted? You told me you were missing him.'

Phyllida flushed. She had forgotten that she had told Chris that. She had only said it was Rupert she was missing because she couldn't say that it was Jake she longed for.

'I was just feeling down about...something else...then,' she explained awkwardly. 'I'm afraid Rupert was just an excuse. When he turned up here, I didn't feel anything for him at all. If anything, it just made me more certain than before that I'd been right to break off our engagement.'

'I see,' said Chris, but she didn't look as if she did.

Phyllida hoped her cousin wasn't about to ask why she had been feeling so down that she'd felt the need of a broken engagement as an excuse. 'When are you planning to go up to the Whitsundays?' she asked brightly.

'As soon as we can sell the house,' said Mike. 'The only problem is letting Jake down. We feel bad about the fact that he's kept Chris's job open for her, but when we told him our plans in the car he was great about it.'

'Frankly, I'm not sure he even took it in,' Chris put in after some reflection. 'He seemed very preoccupied, didn't he, Mike?'

'Perhaps he's got other problems,' Mike suggested. 'Phyllida probably knows. She's the one who's been working with him, after all. What do you think, Phyllida? Has business been good?'

'As far as I know,' she said in a colourless tone. 'It hasn't been so busy this last week, but I think that was expected.'

'How did you and Jake get on, anyway?' asked Chris with interest.

'Fine.' Phyllida's throat was tight, her voice high and brittle.

'Funny, that's what Jake said too,' said Mike humorously. 'He didn't sound as if he meant it either! There's nothing going on between you two, is there?' He laughed heartily at the idea.

'Of course not.' Phyllida tried to smile, but it went rather astray.

Chris had been watching her cousin's face. 'Mike,' she said suddenly, 'don't you think you should go and rest?'

'I'm not tired,' he objected, surprised.

'You've had a long journey, and you haven't been out of hospital long,' said Chris firmly, hauling him to his feet.

While she was chivvying him into the bedroom Phyllida had a chance to rearrange her face and get herself under control again. By the time Chris reappeared, she was sipping her drink with a determinedly cool expression.

Chris sat down beside her. 'Well?'

'Well, what?' said Phyllida, with a fine assumption of nonchalance.

'Well, what's going on between you and Jake?'

'Nothing.'

'Come on, Phyl! I saw your face just now. I can tell something's wrong, and my guess is that it's the same thing that's wrong with Jake.'

'Nothing's wrong,' Phyllida insisted, with an edge of desperation.

'Then why do you look as if you're trying to pretend that your heart's not breaking?'

'It isn't,' she said, but the glass rattled against her teeth as she put it down unsteadily.

'I thought it might be Rupert,' Chris continued inexorably, 'but you tell me it's not. Which leaves Jake—who, coincidentally, is also looking as if he's had a hard kick in the stomach!'

'If he is, it's n-nothing to d-do with m-me,' said Phyllida, and her face crumpled as she lost her battle to control her trembling mouth. 'H-he h-hates me!' Horrified, she put up her hands to cover her face, but it was too late to stop the tears. 'I'm s-sorry,' she sobbed. 'I didn't mean to cry and s-spoil everything for you, just when you're so happy again.'

Chris handed her cousin a tissue. 'I think you'd better tell me all about it,' she said.

Gradually, she coaxed the whole story out of Phyllida. How they had met, how they had argued, how Phyllida had fallen more and more in love with him without knowing it. How the atmosphere had kept changing on that fatal sailing trip and how Jake had been furious with her for walking off on her own. How disagreeable he had been that evening, and then how everything had changed suddenly again.

Phyllida glossed over that night, but presumably Chris got the message, for she nodded understandingly when her cousin told her how devastated she had been by Jake's reaction to the letter he had seen.

'One thing—he sounds even more confused than you were,' she said comfortingly.

'He didn't sound very confused to me,' wept Phyllida. 'He said he didn't want to be part of my life, and then when the boom hit him he was furious!'

Chris had to suppress a smile when Phyllida explained about the goosewing incident. 'If you'd been hit by a boom, you'd be cross too!' she said. 'On the other hand, Jake was probably even angrier because he realised that it was partly his fault for not explaining properly. I don't know what you're worrying about, Phyllida. It sounds to me as if the poor man's out of his mind with jealousy!'

Phyllida shook her head miserably. 'He couldn't wait to get rid of me when Rupert arrived, and anyway—' she sniffed '—he's planning to sail round the world with Val.'

'*What*?' Chris stared at her. 'Who on earth told you that?'

'Val did.'

'Well, I wouldn't believe it until I heard it from Jake,' said Chris stoutly. 'Val's all right, and I dare say Jake's fond of her in his own way, but abandon his business to sail off into the sunset with her? No!'

Phyllida scrubbed her face furiously with the damp and crumpled tissue and refused to be comforted. 'He was there. He heard her say it and he didn't deny it.'

'He probably thought *you* were going to swan off into the sunset with Rupert!' Chris shook her head with mock severity. 'Really, Phyl! I can't believe that two smart, intelligent people like you and Jake could get themselves in such a muddle! You were both wonderful when *I* was in a state, but it doesn't sound to me as if you've the least idea about your own affairs!'

Phyllida opened her mouth to protest, but Chris wouldn't let her speak. 'If you'll take my advice, you'll go straight down to Jake now and tell him what you've just told me.'

'I can't!' she said in panic.

'You can,' said her cousin implacably. 'Do you love him?'

'Yes,' she whispered. 'Yes, I do.'

'Then tell him.' Chris got to her feet. 'If we had a car I'd drive you to the marina, but as it is I'll have to call you a taxi. You go and wash your face.'

'Chris, I don't think—'

But Chris was deaf to Phyllida's flustered objections. She bullied her cousin into getting ready, and personally instructed the taxi driver to take her to the marina and not dare drop her off anywhere else.

Phyllida was borne along by Chris's determination, but as she paid the taxi driver and got out at the marina her courage began to fail her. It had sounded easy when Chris had said that all she had to do was tell Jake she loved him. Now she had no idea where she would begin.

She stood for a while by the wall, looking down over the marina. The sunlight danced and glittered on the water, just as it had done when she had first seen it. The boats still rocked beside the jetty, their gay pennants fluttering proudly in the breeze. The air was as sparkling clear as it had always been. Only she had changed. Slowly, Phyllida walked down the steps to the office.

Jake wasn't there. As she stood there the telephone shrilled loudly, making her jump, but when she moved towards it the answer machine cut in. Jake's voice echoed eerily round the empty office, and Phyllida's heart sank. He only ever put the answer machine on if he was going to be away for a while. Had she come down here for nothing?

From force of habit more than anything else she wandered down the jetty, past the familiar boats rocking comfortably against the pontoons, their mooring lines creaking and the halyards rattling against the masts as the wind caught them. She passed *Valli*, *Persephone*, *Dora Dee*, *Calypso* . . . all gleaming clean in the sunshine. Their decks were scrubbed, their woodwork shining, the guard rails flashing silver.

And then she saw Jake.

He was sitting alone on the *Ali B*, his expression so bleak that Phyllida's heart almost failed her. He had obviously been polishing the brass around the compass in the cockpit, but the rag was forgotten in his hand as he stared out to sea, wrapped in bitter thoughts. He didn't hear Phyllida's footsteps along the pontoon, or know that she was watching him until she spoke.

'Jake?'

His head swung round and he stared at her incredulously, the grey-green eyes ablaze with an emotion Phyllida couldn't identify but which left her tongue-tied and breathless.

'Phyllida,' he said, getting uncertainly to his feet.

There was an agonising silence. It was the first time Phyllida had ever seen him unsure of himself, and she didn't know what to do. She was trapped in a straitjacket of nerves, unable to do more than look helplessly back at him.

She cleared her throat. 'Can I come aboard?' Her voice sounded high and silly to her own ears—too brittle, too English.

'Yes...yes.' Jake seemed to realise that he was still holding the rag and wiped his hands with it as he watched Phyllida step over the guard rails. 'You learnt how to get on board a boat, anyway,' he said.

'Yes.' For want of anything better to do, Phyllida sat down in the cockpit, and Jake subsided slowly opposite her. They didn't seem to be able to do anything but look at each other.

'Where's Rupert?' said Jake, breaking the silence at last.

'He's gone.'

'I thought you were going with him?' He sounded strained, and Phyllida moistened her lips.

'He asked me to, but I...I decided to stay.'

'Why?' he asked harshly. 'You want to go back to your career in England. You want Rupert. He's perfect for you...successful, sophisticated, prepared to come all this way to apologise to you.' His voice was very bitter. 'You belong together.'

'That's what I used to think, but I don't belong with Rupert any more.' Phyllida drew a deep breath and looked directly at Jake. 'I belong here,' she said.

Jake went very still. He stared back at her as if her words were filtering slowly through to him, and then the defeated look drained from his face as an incredulous smile lit his eyes. 'You want to stay?'

She nodded, and he reached for her hands and drew her to her feet with him. 'You want to stay here?' he asked, still sounding as if he couldn't quite believe what he was hearing.

'Yes.'

'With me?'

'Yes...if you'll have me.'

'Have you?' Jake gave a sudden, exuberant shout of laughter. 'I've been sitting here in black despair because I thought you'd gone and that I'd never see you again, and you ask if I'll have you!' His hands tightened around hers and he smiled down into her eyes.

'I've been cursing myself as every kind of fool for letting you go to Rupert, and wondering if I'd be too late if I followed you to England and begged you to come back, but I thought you'd refuse. I'd have been asking you to give up your career and your flat and your smart lifestyle, and I knew I couldn't give you any of the things you'd said you wanted.'

'I don't want them any more,' said Phyllida as the cold stone of misery and despair shattered and dissolved in an explosion of exquisite relief that the pretence was over and she could tell him the truth at last. 'I only want you.'

And then she was in his arms, and he was kissing her, and she clung to him and kissed him back, as if afraid that the wondering happiness would vanish if she stopped. It was Jake who drew back first, and Phyllida caught her breath at the expression in his eyes. He took her face between hands that shook slightly, and looked down at her as no man had ever looked at her before.

'I love you,' he said seriously, although the smile still glimmered. 'Do you really love me, Phyllida?'

'Yes,' she said on a half-sob, tears of happiness trembling on the ends of her lashes. The sudden release from the tension and distress of the last few days had left her feeling quite dizzy. 'Oh, yes, I do!'

'And you'll marry me? You'll stay for ever?'

'Yes, yes,' she said, half laughing, half crying, and pulled his head down so that she could kiss him again.

Much later, she leant back against him as they sat close together in the cockpit, and sighed happily at the feel of Jake's arms wrapped securely around her. 'I've been so miserable,' she told him. 'I thought you despised me.'

'I tried to,' Jake admitted. 'The first time I saw you, in that smart suit of yours, I thought you would be like Jonelle—obsessed with your image and your career. I didn't want to get involved with anyone like that again, and all the alarm bells went off whenever you mentioned your job, but no matter how hard I tried not to, I couldn't help noticing that you *weren't* like Jonelle.' He stroked her hair, a tousled mop now, rather than an immaculately swinging bob, but still soft and still shining.

'Jonelle wouldn't have given up her plans for anyone, and she certainly wouldn't have got down on her hands and knees to scrub decks. I worked you much harder than I should have done, I know. I think I almost wanted you to give up, and convince me that you were like Jonelle after all, because then it would have been easier for me to ignore how bright your eyes were and how your whole face lit up when you laughed.'

He smiled, twisting a strand of hair round one finger. 'But you wouldn't give up, would you? There was something gallant about the way you refused to let yourself be beaten. I was rude to you, I bullied and provoked you, but you just stuck your chin in the air and glared right back at me.

'Jonelle was much more subtle. She used to rely on feminine wiles to get her own way. She could be sweetness itself when it suited her, but it was only to disguise her iron will. You were so much more honest. At first I told myself that I secretly admired your defiance, and then I realised that what I felt for you was a lot stronger than admiration.'

'I was convinced you thought I was absolutely ridiculous!'

'I have to admit that you *did* amuse me. You were so stubborn, so determined to be contrary.' Jake's voice changed, and he ran his finger caressingly down her cheek. 'And so beautiful.'

Phyllida shivered beneath his touch. 'I didn't think I was your type. I thought you liked long-legged blondes?'

'Not any more,' said Jake, kissing the sensitive spot just below her ear. 'My taste is for small, fiery brunettes, with elfin faces and the sweetest kisses...' His lips drifted along her jaw and she turned her head with a smile so that they could claim her mouth.

'The first time I kissed you was just an impulse,' he murmured after a while. 'I wasn't prepared for the effect it would have on me, or for the fact that I couldn't get it out of my mind. I was falling more and more in love with you, but I fought it every inch of the way. Jonelle made me very wary of love.'

'I didn't want to fall in love either,' Phyllida said, snuggling closer against him. 'After Rupert, I was determined to be independent.'

'That's what I thought,' he said. 'You talked about your career, and what you would do when you got home, and it made me realise that Australia was just a temporary phase for you. I kept forgetting, though. When I kissed you, when we walked along the beach, when we sat together in the darkness...it seemed so *right*.

'I nearly gave in that night at Reevesby, but you started talking about going home to your job, and I decided it was pointless. I didn't want a temporary affair, and I thought that the more involved I got, the more I'd regret it in the end. It didn't stop me feeling extremely frustrated, though!'

'Is that why you were so foul to me the next day?'

'I'm afraid so. I even shunted you off to the beach at Memory Cove because I was terrified I wouldn't be able to keep my hands off you any longer. And then, of course, I lost control completely when I looked round to see that you'd disappeared! If it had been anyone else, I'd have assumed they'd gone for a walk and left them to it, but, because it was you, I rushed off to try and find you and make sure you were all right.'

'I'm glad you did,' said Phyllida. 'It was so stupid of me to try and get down to that beach, but it was a sort of test for myself, to see if I'd be able to live without you...and I failed it dismally. I knew then that I was stuck with loving you, but of course you were furious with me, and it all seemed more hopeless than ever.'

'I said a lot of things I shouldn't,' Jake apologised with a rueful grin. 'But I was so afraid when I saw you lying down there. Everything went black until I got you back on the track and saw that you really were all right, and then I lost my head. I was furious with you for giving me such a scare, and even more furious with myself for caring so much if you were even slightly scratched.'

'I wish I'd known,' sighed Phyllida, resting her head back against his shoulder. 'I was so miserable that evening!'

'Is that why you spent the whole time flirting with everybody except me?'

She blushed faintly. 'I didn't want you to guess how much I loved you,' she explained, and he kissed her.

'It worked,' he said, raising his head. 'I was so jealous I couldn't think straight! I couldn't think about anything except how much I wanted you, and when we got back on the boat... Well, I just lost what little self-control I had left.'

She smiled at the memory, and felt his arms close more firmly around her. 'It was so wonderful,' she remembered softly. 'Couldn't you tell how much I loved you then?'

'I let myself hope you did. I even let myself think that everything would be all right after all—and then I saw that you'd written to Rupert, and I decided I'd been making a complete fool of myself. I was angry with myself for falling so deeply in love with you, and humiliated at the idea that I'd let you see it when it seemed as if you were still interested in Rupert.'

Phyllida sat up in surprise. 'I had no idea,' she protested. 'All I knew was that you'd suddenly gone cold on me.'

'I thought it would be easiest if I put a stop to things there and then,' said Jake. 'It served me right when you knocked me out with the boom!'

'I didn't do it deliberately!'

'I know.' He grinned. 'And anyway, it didn't hurt nearly as much as when I overheard you telling Chris that you were missing Rupert. I'd got up to answer the phone and was just about to open the door when you started talking.

'I'm ashamed to say I listened, hoping against hope that I'd learn something about what you felt after that night, but you know what they say about eaves-droppers...! I was devastated when you said that it was Rupert you were thinking about, not me. It just confirmed everything I was most afraid of.'

'I only said that because I didn't want to tell her I was crazy about you.'

Jake pulled her back into the circle of his arms. 'Why didn't you tell me?'

'Why didn't *you* tell *me*?' countered Phyllida, and he gave a wry smile.

'Stupid pride, I suppose. I avoided you as much as I could, certain that you were making plans to go back to Rupert, but then, when he turned up, I was poleaxed with jealousy! He was just the sort of man I'd expected you to have, and he fitted your image in a way I knew I'd never do.'

Phyllida touched his cheek lovingly. 'Maybe he did once, but I've changed since I met you. Even Chris noticed that I was different!'

Jake held her away from him slightly, as if comparing the career girl he had met at Adelaide airport, in her gold shoes and her matching accessories, with the girl smiling at him now, careless of her appearance, her only

ornament the wide eyes that were shining and starry with
love. 'Maybe you have changed, at that!' He smiled.

'Or maybe I was like this all along, and I just didn't
know it,' said Phyllida. 'I knew as soon as Rupert arrived that I'd never really loved him—not the way I loved
you—but I didn't think it was fair to tell him five minutes
after he'd got off the plane.'

'Is that why you told Val you were engaged?'

'I didn't,' she said indignantly. '*You* were the one who
told her that, not me!'

Jake shifted uncomfortably. 'Well, you didn't deny
it.'

'How could I? I'd promised Rupert I'd think about
it, and I could hardly smash his hopes in front of an
audience. Anyway,' Phyllida went on, remembering, 'I
didn't think it would make much difference to you. I
thought you'd been involved with Val all along, and had
just been amusing yourself with me.'

'With *Val*?' Jake looked astonished. 'What on earth
made you think that?'

'Well, what was this round-the-world trip you were
planning together?' she asked accusingly, and his brow
cleared.

'The only thing we were doing together was the
planning, you idiot! Val's determined to sail round the
world single-handed, and I was just supposed to be giving
her advice about the supplies she'd need—not that I made
a single sensible suggestion once you and Rupert appeared! I could hardly eat, I was so choked with
jealousy.' Jake gave another wry grin.

'I hadn't realised I had such primitive impulses.
Jonelle made me feel sad and bitter, but I'd never felt
the sheer rage I felt seeing you and Rupert together. I
wanted to choke the life out of him for daring to touch

you, and then drag you off so that I could somehow manage to beat you and make love to you at the same time!'

He shook his head. 'And all the time you thought I was interested in Val! How could you even *think* that?'

'She's got long legs,' Phyllida explained, slightly on the defensive. 'And she knows all about sailing.'

'True, but the ability to tell a boom from a bilge pump isn't much competition for a pair of stormy brown eyes,' Jake pointed out, amused. 'Val's a nice girl, and I like her a lot, but I wouldn't want to spend a year in a boat with her.'

'That's what Chris said,' she admitted.

'Oh, you've talked to Chris, have you?' he teased.

'I was busy denying everything, but she wormed the truth out of me in the end. She sent me down here with strict instructions not to go back until we'd both stopped being so silly!' Phyllida smiled. 'She said it was obvious that you were in love with me.'

'Wise Chris!' said Jake, kissing her hair. 'Shall we go and tell her how right she was?'

Phyllida disentangled herself from him with some reluctance and got up, stretching with sheer delight.

The sky was a deep cobalt blue, and the sunshine dazzled her eyes. Everything was brighter, sharper, more distinct—as if glinting with reflected joy—and even the water murmuring against the boats and the breeze chinking the rigging seemed like a chuckling echo of her happiness.

Smiling, she kissed Jake again, and they walked hand in hand along the jetty to break the good news to Chris and Mike.

Less than three hours later, they were back at the marina. A delighted Chris had urged them to stay and celebrate, but Jake and Phyllida had had other plans, and as the afternoon light softened into evening gold, the *Ali B* nosed her way out of the marina, unfurled her sails and headed south towards Memory Cove.

* * * * * *

And a child that's born on a Sunday
Is bonny and blithe and good and gay!
Look out next month for Helen Brooks'
Dream Wedding, the final book in
our exciting series.